DARK PROVIDENCE

Bright Promise

BY KEN LEECH

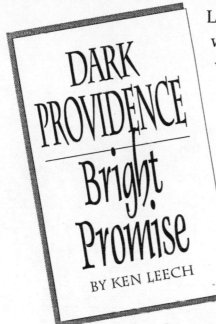

Dark Providence, Bright Promise

by Ken Leech

Light and Life PRESS
Indianapolis, IN

DARK PROVIDENCE, BRIGHT PROMISE
by Ken Leech

ISBN 0-89367-196-7

Originally published by
Christian Witness Crusades, Lancashire, England,
under the title *True Witness — The Amazing Story of Detective Leech*

© 1995 reprint
by Light and Life Press,
Indianapolis, IN 46253-5002
Printed in the U.S.A

To Charles W. Kingsley,
Director of Christian Witness Crusades
Light and Life Men International
Free Methodist Church of North America,
the inspiration behind this book.

And,

To

His Followers Everywhere,
May the sharing of my once desperate dilemma
encourage you to be bold for Christ's sake.
While hesitant Christians wait — dedicated cults
and false religions reap the harvest.

"Open your eyes and look at the fields!
They are ripe for harvest."

John 4:35, NIV

"We are all witnesses."

Acts 2:32, NIV

Contents

Foreword

written for _True Witness_ *

I first met Ken Leech in September of 1973, 15 months after his remarkable conversion. I was amazed at his keen insight into the spiritual and his grasp of the Scriptures as we shared together in visitation to homes already invaded by cults.

It was my privilege to be present the Sunday evening when Ken announced his decision to prepare for the ministry in a total way. A year later he entered London Bible College taking with him the alertness of a detective searching the Holy Scriptures.

Ken and Joan Leech dedicated their summer vacation in 1975 to visiting America for the first time to share their exciting faith and dramatic experiences. They visited eight states and Ontario, Canada, making a real spiritual impact. Their challenge was two-fold:

First — the comfortable church was urged not to surrender the white fields of their communities to the zealous cults.

Second — Christians were encouraged to make the full commitment and find their place of exciting fulfillment in these days of tremendous opportunity for His church.

Ken and Joan, accompanied by their three sons, Kenneth, John and Stephen (then 14, 12 and 10) returned to North America for twelve months of experience with Christian Witness Crusades. They returned to England in August of 1977 to pioneer the planting of new churches beginning with their present assignment in the Fulwood area of Preston. Their ministry to our continent was indeed most encouraging for which we give God the glory.

Charles W. Kingsley, Director
Christian Witness Crusades

Ken Leech has a mind like a steel trap. As a detective NOTHING escapes his notice.

In viewing this manuscript for publication, I have been fascinated to watch as a hardnosed detective becomes a convinced disciple of a false cult, then a very loyal follower of Jesus Christ.

We get a first-hand account of the inner workings of a British Police Force. Then we catch the unmistakable glory of God's matchless grace transforming a Sergeant of its Criminal Investigation Department into a dynamic witness of the Eternal Truth.

Howard A. Snyder
Executive Director
Light and Life Men International

* Originally published by
Christian Witness Crusades, Lancashire, England,
under the title *True Witness — The Amazing Story of Detective Leech*

Tragedy and Triumph
Preface

by U. Milo Kaufmann
President, Light and Life Men International

Planes waiting to land at Chicago's O'Hare International Airport sweep out great circles 60 miles or more in radius. American Eagle Flight 4184, en route to Chicago from Indianapolis on the evening of Monday, October 31, 1994, and 32 minutes into a holding pattern, found itself over northwestern Indiana when the first signs of serious trouble appeared. One wing dipped, and the autopilot compensated. The two pilots were quick and competent, but the conditions were most difficult. At 10,000 feet the temperature was below freezing. The rain was heavy. Wind gusts were treacherous.

What happened next will never be fully understood, but the outline of events can be reconstructed. The wing that had already dipped dipped again, and the plane flipped onto its back.

Experienced pilots will say that flying while upside down presents its own challenges. Stunt pilots, of course, can do it briefly. But the trimming of the plane's flight surfaces must be reversed. The evidence is that the plane's two propjet engines were still running when the plane flew into the ground just moments later. The plane rammed the ground with such force that only small fragments remained from the impact. The largest recovered piece of the plane was a 6-foot by 4-foot section of the tail. Bodies of the 64 passengers and four crew members on board were all but atomized, making the identification process difficult. (In time, though, all *were* identified.)

The plane was at about 8,000 feet when it disappeared from Air Traffic Control radar at O'Hare Airport. A plane cruising at 300 miles per hour would cover 8,000 feet on the horizontal in about 18 seconds. If it is vectored toward the ground, the gravity-assist shortens the time. Whatever the interval between first warning and impact, it was not adequate for the necessary compensations as the pilots took the plane off autopilot and struggled gamely to right the plane.

Perhaps the 64 passengers on American Eagle Flight 4184 had a full minute to think and pray while the crew fought to keep the plane aloft. What must have passed through their minds? First of all, one supposes, there was the numbness of complete helplessness. Then the awkwardness of being suspended from the floor and seats, now becoming the ceiling and unsecured items lurching from side to side. Add to this the uncertainty about location with respect to the ground. Then the impact, and nothingness. What remains is the aching emptiness of those who have lost loved ones, valued work associates, longtime friends.

The 64 passengers on Flight 4184 comprised a diverse and international group. A couple from Sweden, in their seventies, had been in Indianapolis to visit a daughter. A young businessman from Korea had attended an Industrial Fabrics Association meeting in Indianapolis and was traveling to Chicago to visit a brother. A professor at Northeastern Illinois University had plans to return to his native South Africa to help shape the teaching of music there. The flight also included at least four people from the United Kingdom. Among these were Ken Leech and his associate Alan Ramm.

These last two would not have supposed that only nothingness follows that last breath, the final flicker of light. They were devoted Christians, persuaded that death is never, for anyone, the final moment. Persuaded, too, they would have been, that in the darkest of moments God is yet, somehow, working out His providential ends.

The substance of the book that follows is the gripping life story of Ken Leech as he put it into writing himself some time ago. Ken's life was marked by a number of what we might call dark providences. The grisly event which put him on a serious adult quest for spiritual truth was the rape and murder of a 17-year-old Sunday school teacher. When Ken was assigned to the case, in charge of developing background data on all the men who might have known the victim, he was a tough, ambitious Lancashire policeman, ignorant of the transforming power of the living Jesus Christ. One thing that registered strongly with him was the peace and forgiving spirit of the murdered girl's parents. They had a trust in Providence far beyond anything Ken found to be natural. Ken's account of his rising through the ranks of a crack Lancashire police force is a vivid one, told with an eye for the significant detail — exactly what we would expect from a detective.

And his police career was spent with a very fine outfit indeed. In one of the latter years of Ken's time in criminal investigation, the whole of Lancashire had a total of only some 20 murders. As if that fact were not astonishing enough to those who are now accustomed to murder reports in every evening newspaper, the further wonder is that all but one of those murders were solved. (The exception was the case of a woman who operated a sidewalk kiosk and was slain by a hit-and-skip intruder who managed to lose himself in the crowd.)

Yet, Ken would say that the grandest wonder of his life was how he was found by a loving God. With conversion came a clear call to another sort of warfare against the forces which destroy human persons. Under God's call he became a coura-geous evangelist, ever ready to take up the challenge in a new place, including the magical far edges of Cornwall, not far from Land's End.

Ken's own account of the mighty acts of God in and through him ends in the mid-70s. His colleague and friend, Reverend Colin Le Noury of Preston, Lancashire, supplies two closing chapters. They document how many good things were brought full circle in Ken's life and work.

Sudden Death — Sudden Fear
Chapter One

I had not been at Fleetwood many weeks when the weather-beaten, battle-scarred Sergeant said to me, "Now then, son," (I suppose that was all I was to him, just a raw youngster barely 19 years old) "have you reported a sudden death yet?"

"No, Sergeant, I haven't," I replied.

He gave a deep chuckle and grinned almost wickedly at me. He was a somber individual, and this was a rare display of cheerfulness. The albino scar on his right cheek cut a jagged furrow into his craggy features.

"'There's no time like the present. You've got one now," he said.

I shuddered inwardly as I visualized the scene very shortly to be enacted before me.

My thoughts went back to February of that year, to a bitterly cold, mist-shrouded day when a Silver City Airways Bristol 170 aeroplane on its way from the Isle of Man to the city of Manchester had plowed into the snow-covered crest of 'Winter Hill,' almost 1500 feet above sea level, killing 35 of its 42 passengers. The first officer had managed to stagger 350 yards to the Independent Television Authority's transmitting station to raise the alarm. The solitary winding road which led up through the bleak moorland to this desolate spot had been enveloped by drifting snow sealing off the building from the outside world. Bulldozers and snowplows were needed to clear the way for the rapidly assembled rescue teams.

The grim carnage awaiting them was horrifying even to the most seasoned veterans. I recalled stories of how dismembered corpses were painstakingly carried on ambulance emergency stretchers over extremely hazardous terrain to reach the waiting rescue vehicles several hundred feet below. I vividly recalled the expression on one young police officer's face as he retched and vomited involuntarily in the Police Station, after returning from one of the postmortem examinations being carried out in an adjacent church schoolroom, which had been converted into a temporary mortuary.

I had not actually seen any of the dead bodies myself, but I had studied intently the detective sergeant who had been sent over from the Isle of Man to identify their remains. He had known them all personally since his school days. After carrying out formal identifications at the temporary mortuary he came back into the police station. A handkerchief was wrapped tightly around one of his fists, and both hands were clenched so that the whites of his knuckles showed. He pounded the wooden top of the charge office desk, and his burly frame shook visibly. He seemed incapable of speech — then he slowly and deliberately began to bang his head against the office wall.

I shuddered to think of what sights he must have seen to cause him to behave in such a manner. I was only a Police Cadet at the time, and my only direct connection with the incident (apart from pairing together and cleaning a room full of very dirty, mud-streaked shoes) was connected with the coffins. All the bodies had been placed in coffins and aligned in rows, lying on top of wooden planks laid across the tops of the pews in the adjoining church. I had to check the gleaming brass name plates to ensure that all the names had been rightly inscribed.

My mind was suddenly jolted back to the situation before

me. Inwardly I cursed the day I had joined the police force. I wished myself a thousand miles away from the Lancashire Constabulary and the sudden death which was the inevitable lot of a cop, but it could not be. I tried to appear cool and calm. I spoke in what I considered to be a nonchalant manner. I was determined not to show my fear before this seasoned campaigner if I could help it. I detested the thought of someone recognizing a weakness in my makeup.

A few hours later, I was driven from Fleetwood to Thornton-Cleveleys in a black Vauxhall patrol car, a distance of some five miles or so. I was deposited on the front step of the mortuary and left to my own devices. The building itself was a modern one set in pleasant surroundings with verdant trees and shrubs and brightly colored flower beds. Its appearance certainly belied its purpose. It was a beautiful day. I looked up at an azure sky. A light golden sun gently radiated warmth all around, but I knew the world I was about to enter was far removed from all this. How inescapable the reality of death and the unknown world beyond. I took a deep breath, plucked up what little courage I could muster and opened the door. I strode in as though I was in complete command of the situation.

I walked along a short corridor to the scene of operations. The actual room was no more than a barren cubicle. The naked corpse of a middle-aged woman lay on a white marble slab. Two men were standing near the far corner of the room — the mortuary attendant and the pathologist. The attendant, who was by far the older of the two, was fastening the tapes to secure the rubber apron which the pathologist had donned in preparation for his task.

Both men had been standing with their backs to me and on turning around the pathologist saw me and smiled pleasantly.

"Good afternoon, officer. We are all ready for you. Before I start would you please tell me about the circumstances surrounding this woman's death?" He spoke as though he was discussing a children's Sunday school outing to the seaside!

As I outlined the facts to him, I tried to figure out what kind of man he must be to engage in such a morbid occupation. He opened his small black case and selected a scalpel. It looked so small and insignificant. I watched him, absolutely fascinated, desperately wanting to pull my eyes away and look elsewhere, anywhere, but I was utterly unable to do so. He leaned over the body and began his incision just below the chin.

Forty minutes later (it had seemed like an eternity to me) he said, "Officer, have you got your tape measure with you please? I want to measure the length of the body."

I took from my hip pocket the little black pouch containing the yellow tape measure and removed it. He held one end, and I held the other.

"Five feet four inches. Thank you, officer," he said. As he handed his end of the tape back to me it slipped from his fingers and into the gaping, wide open body. I quickly pulled it clear, trying to make sure I didn't touch that part of the tape which was now daubed with thick red blood. I shuddered. "Sorry about that," he said, again smiling benignly at me. Again I wondered what kind of man could be so carefree about this gruesome profession.

By this time I was reaching my breaking point. I could feel my knees beginning to buckle. The color of my face paled. I broke out into a cold sweat. I vainly sought to draw in fresh air, but with each gasping breath I just swallowed more of the all-prevailing stench of death. I turned abruptly around and staggered for the door. I almost made it, but then I stumbled and fell headlong in front of it. My helmet fell off my head and rolled on the floor. I grabbed it and clutched it to my chest. Still on my knees, I pushed the door open and crawled out, not daring to look back to see what the two men thought of my theatrical performance.

Somehow, I don't know how, I got back down the corridor

and out the front door. I sucked in huge quantities of life-giving fresh air. Nothing ever seemed so precious! As I started to revive, I imagined what the two men in the mortuary must be thinking of me — probably grinning at each other and winking broadly. How many times had they seen rookie coppers do this? Or was I the first? I felt I would never be able to face them again, but face them I must. If I was going to be able to hold my head up again before them it had to be then and there. I turned resolutely around and went back in.

The grizzly task was now completed. The pathologist was scrubbing himself up in the sink. Neither of the two men said anything when I returned, or gave any indication that anything unusual had occurred.

"Death was due to natural causes, officer," he said. "I'll make out my report for the coroner tomorrow."

A thought came into my mind, a question which became uppermost in my thinking and burned deep inside. What is life all about? What is the purpose in living? What is the purpose of life itself? Try as I might I could not answer that question. As I walked up the road to the nearby local police station I said to myself. "How long will it be before that ghoul of a pathologist is cutting into me with his deadly scalpel?"

My thought patterns persisted in this vein. What was the difference between a live person and a dead body? What had happened to the life-giving force that had once made that lady warm and tender and which now left her cold and stiff? Was death the cessation of existence? Or was there a life hereafter?

To me, these were questions with no answers. The haunting fear of death was to be my constant companion for the next 13 years!

"My heart is in anguish within me; the terrors of death assail me" (Psalms 55:4, NIV).

Reality and Reminiscence

Chapter Two

I arrived at Fleetwood on the 28th of June, 1958, my 19th birthday. It was my first "posting" as a constable, and my new uniform bore the freshly issued collar number 2824. The first three numbers were coincidentally the same as my parents' telephone number. I took this as a good omen for my career as a "copper."

I had undergone three months training at the No. 1 District Police Training Center at Bruche near the town of Warrington. There I had been taught that the primary duties of a policeman were the protection of life and property; the prevention and detection of crime; and the keeping of the Queen's peace. At the concluding ceremony I was awarded the joint highest percentage of marks in the final examinations of the course. This distinction had not been gained easily, but I had studied tenaciously to the rigid exclusion of other pastimes and pleasures. I had read the forward of the book we were to be tested over with eager anticipation and had come across these words: "On the beat live people of all creeds and varying stations of life, but to the police officer, so far as his duty to the public is concerned, all are equal and equally entitled to his protection." The book then cited the following quotation: "'True liberty can only exist when justice is equally administered to all — to the king and to the beggar' — Chief Justice Mansfield." I resolved to uphold this cardinal principle of British justice with all my might and main.

I had then undergone a two weeks "local procedure" course at Stanley Grange, which was then Lancashire Constabulary's training center. The center was comprised of a large country house which had been converted into an administrative block. On the grounds had been erected a collection of wooden huts, some of which were used as classrooms and others as sleeping quarters. It was rather primitive. But for all that, it has held many happy memories for literally thousands of new recruits who have passed through its portals over the years. Many had gone out to perform glorious service for King, Queen and country and had brought fame and honor to the force. I was one of the last groups of policemen to pass through its precincts, and I remember feeling distinctly proud of the privilege of being a member of this very fine constabulary. My determination was to uphold the traditions of those who had gone before me.

I reported directly to the police station, and the duty sergeant was informed of my presence. He took me to 25 Burns Road, which was to be my home for the next fifteen months. On the way there, he told me that this house had not been used for lodgings by the police previously and that the occupant, a Mrs. Nellie Buckley, had in fact never accommodated a lodger of any kind, and therefore the quality and character of the abode and person were unknown factors.

The sergeant rang the doorbell, and we both waited for the front door to open. When it did, a middle-aged, grey haired woman let out a loud exclamation and said, "Oh, he's just like our Billy."

I learned afterwards that "Billy" was one of her sons who had been lost at sea while following his occupation as a trawlerman. From that moment she treated me like a long lost son and, on finding out that my two favorite dishes were rice pudding and pancakes, she lavishly treated me to abundant helpings of them every week without fail.

The town of Fleetwood itself, comprising some 29,000 people, is situated on the west coast of Lancashire, a few miles north of the famous holiday resort of Blackpool. It is predominantly a fishing port with its tourist industry as a secondary source of income during the summer months. The trawlermen lead extremely dangerous lives, braving the Icelandic seas in all weathers. Many men and boats have been lost without trace over its short but proud history.

Later I vividly recalled one fog-shrouded night in early December, 1959, standing on the pier jetty shortly after midnight watching three trawlers, which had been tied up alongside each other, slip their moorings one by one and glide silently almost ghostlike out of the harbor on the outgoing high tide, disappearing eerily into the unseen beyond. I was unable to identify them at the time, the fog having reduced visibility to almost zero. But later I had cause to believe that one of them was named the "Red Falcon," a trawler of some 449 tons. I was probably the very last person in Fleetwood to see that vessel and crew depart on the way to a watery grave, never to return. On the 14th of December, while on its way back from Icelandic seas, it was lost with all hands.

No trace was ever found of the vessel or her 19-man crew. One of the senior constables in the police canteen on reading of the tragedy in the newspaper said bitterly, "Nineteen men lost and we've never even locked one of them up. Why is it always the good that die young? I could have filled that boat with nineteen men no one would have missed!"

Cynical and cruel maybe, but everyone in the room understood his frustration and the grief contained in those poignant sentences.

Mrs. Buckley told me she dreaded the month of December, for it almost always brought tragic loss of life to both her own family and to the town. The men never knew whether the next trip was going to be their last, so if and when they made it safely back to port many of them determined to make the most of it. They usually had very short periods of time ashore before they were due to set sail again for distant waters. Those who successfully returned with good catches were rewarded with a fistful of money which they endeavored to spend in the shortest possible time, painting the town red with wine, women and song. They often collided with the forces of law and order! I well remember a saying of my then mother-in-law to be: "When the drink is in, the wit is out." She was only repeating a well-known quotation, but how true it was and still is.

My first day on duty, I was put with a more experienced constable. Our beat included the notorious Dock Street, a long, straight road running along the railway track and the docks where the unmistakable odor of fish filled the air daily. Here the human dregs of Fleetwood gathered to booze, gossip and gamble. Here the homeless slept in the Seaman's Mission or in the common lodging, if they could afford it. When they couldn't, they slept on the cold, hard floor of public latrines or in a backstreet entranceway with only the cacophony of stray cats for company.

Following in the wake of this sea of human debris was a small corps of part-time prostitutes. Some suggested there weren't more because while many of the husbands were at sea, some of the wives lived openly with other men. Such clandestine cohabitation was not uncommon. This was certainly not the pattern for the whole town, however. In the two years I served in Fleetwood I grew to greatly admire the fortitude, gritty determination and unswerving loyalty of the fishermen and their families. Such was the family of my landlady, Nellie Buckley, and her kin.

My very first day I made two arrests — both out-of-work trawlermen. One was arrested for being drunk and incapable. The poor chap was lying completely flat out at 3:00 p.m., his head and shoulders spread over the gutter and into the roadway. He presented an inviting target for passing motorists with his feet turned up motionless on the pavement. He was absolutely stoned to the eyeballs from a mixture of cheap red wine (known as "plonk") and a well-known brand of firegrate polish. The second man was arrested for being drunk and disorderly and for using indecent language. He was causing considerable disturbance and annoyance to pedestrians as they passed by. Failing to heed a solemn warning to behave himself and make his way quietly home — which he greeted with a torrent of abuse and a barrage of four-letter words — he was promptly locked up. My second day I gave evidence in Court before the local Magistrates. Since it was not permitted to repeat out loud the obscenities uttered, I had the quite amusing experience of completing my evidence by saying, "I told him to be quiet and to go home peaceably, your Worship, to which he replied ..." — and I then handed the Magistrates slips of paper on which his reply had been typed out. It was most amusing to watch the expressions change on their faces as they read the typed reply. A copy of his reply was also given to the defendant, who, on reading it, hung his head shamefully.

About the fourth day I was assigned a bicycle beat on the outskirts of the town. The Sergeant notified me that I would be patrolling on my own. I hadn't the courage to tell him I didn't yet have a bicycle, but one of my colleagues lent me his. I had a map of the town and a beat schedule giving the times when I had to be in specific places.

Along the route I suddenly realized I needed to visit a restroom — but how to find one in a strange neighborhood? Finally I spotted one, a nice, modern-looking building. Inside was a pay toilet, but to my surprise the door was ajar. I could have entered without paying, but as yet I was not too tainted with the ways of the world so I promptly closed the door, deposited my coin, and entered legally.

Moments later I found to my horror that the door wouldn't open! No matter how hard I tried, it refused to budge. I panicked. How long was I going to be stuck here? This was a semirural part of town, and perhaps no one would come in for hours. And even if someone did come, would my pride let me call for help? I was in full uniform, helmet and all, and wouldn't I look ridiculous if someone had to put a penny in the slot to rescue the patrolling constable!

I looked desperately around me, and then I saw above the door there was not the usual glass panel, but a wire meshing. I stood on the toilet seat and reached out and pushed against it. It was quite solid and didn't budge. I pulled out my truncheon (billy club), wrapped the leather thong firmly round my wrist and began to hammer away at the meshing. It was stubborn, but my persistence gained reward and with a cry of triumph I knocked the wire covering away from its supports. It fell through on the far side of the door.

I looked at the opening above me and wondered how I was going to get through it. Not with my helmet on that was for sure! I took it off and threw it through the opening. Then I decided my truncheon would also be a hindrance to me, so that followed in the wake of my helmet. I then sprang from the toilet seat and hauled myself up, getting my head and shoulders through the gap. Then I dived headlong and did a forward roll on the other side, finishing up at the feet of a small boy who had just entered the toilets and obviously couldn't believe his eyes! I picked up my truncheon, put my helmet squarely on my head, and fastened the chin strap. I surveyed the damage I had caused and then left in as authoritative a manner as I could muster before the small, incredulous pair of eyes and gaping mouth of the youngster. I mounted the bike and rode briskly away.

My thoughts raced furiously. Before long, some well-meaning citizen would report the damage to the station. Perhaps that young boy was already on his way home to tell his mum. Before I knew it, the Criminal Investigation Department (C.I.D.) would be on my trail. There was only one course of action to take and that was to inform my sergeant. The thought of this made me squirm, but I had no alternative. As soon as I got into the station I made a beeline for the sergeant and politely asked him to one side as I recounted my tale of woe. He roared with unrestrained laughter until his sides itched!

"Ginger," he said, addressing me, "those toilets are brand spanking new. They haven't even been officially opened yet. The Mayor is due to do that next Saturday." Again he roared into uncontrollable laughter. When he eventually quieted down, he said in a fatherly manner, "Leave it to me. Ginger, I'll contact the foreman in charge and have it put right before the Mayor gets there."

I don't know what he told the foreman, but I never heard another word about the episode and everything was "ship shape and in Bristol fashion" for the Lord Mayor's official opening that Saturday.

Most of my duties, however, were on the town beats, and over the next few weeks I very quickly learned the art of arresting drunken trawlermen who persisted in their lawbreaking. Offenses commonly included drunkenness, fighting in the street, urinating, indecent language and depositing litter (mainly empty 'plonk' bottles) in the streets.

In sharp contrast to its Dock Street image, Fleetwood had another facet to its character. This was the tourist industry. During the short summer months, hundreds of motorists would arrive in the town, many on a purely daily basis, converging on the Esplanade where they would take advantage of the recreational facilities. These included a large open-air swimming pool and bandstand, bowling and putting greens, a yachting lake and boating pool, and a variety of children's amusements.

Late one night as I was patrolling the tourist area tragedy struck the North Euston Hotel. I heard the fire brigade rapidly approaching and, as it roared past, I set off after it and arrived at the scene to find the North Euston ablaze. People were standing on upstairs window ledges, some in total panic, and smoke was pouring out.

The fire brigade did a magnificent job. There was only one fatality, a man who had been overcome by smoke fumes. I was present with the inspector at the nearby hospital shortly after the body had been recovered. The man was laid out naked on a stretcher. The hands were hanging incongruously over the sides. The inspector folded them neatly over the chest, but they promptly slid off and hung limply. The inspector tried again, but with the same result. Finally the night nurse, seeing our predicament, showed us what to do by tucking the arms under the body.

This man had been wealthy, but met his fate suddenly and unexpectedly at a time when he must have been feeling very secure in the comfort and warmth of Fleetwood's plushest hotel. My experiences were beginning to tell me that no one was immune from the clutches of death. Whether young or old, rich or poor. The grim reaper takes his toll on all mankind, and I knew that the only thing I could be certain of in life was the fact that the handwriting on the wall was for me. My mind again asked the gnawing question, "How long will it be before I am lying lifeless in some impersonal hospital mortuary and taking no further interest in the world around?" It was a sobering thought to realize there was no possible way of escape, for me or anyone else!

After a few months service I was put on station duty for two weeks as part of my probationary two-year training program. This meant assisting one of the senior constables, answering and dealing with the telephone switchboard and teleprinter circulations, and attending to the many inquiries of the general public. It also gave one the opportunity of regular day-time shifts. This was rather welcome for most of us, but brought along with it added responsibility and what could only be described on occasions as bedlam! Far too often for comfort one would simultaneously encounter the shrill voice of the telephone, the seemingly incessant chatter of the teleprinter (for which there always appeared to be a backlog of messages waiting to be circulated) and the unending line of visitors at the public counter. People's needs ranged from the sublime to the ridiculous, from wanting to know if we had found their pet mongrel dog which answered to the name of 'Rover,' to asking for details about the next Preston Guild, which is only held every twenty years. One never knew what was going to be asked next, and it was a test of one's ingenuity to send people away fully satisfied without having to seek recourse to the sergeant.

Through all these experiences, except for my fear of death, I thoroughly enjoyed my police work. The months flew by at almost breakneck speed. I was now familiar with every street, factory, business and shop in the whole town, and I knew by sight and name regular troublemakers who frequented the back alleys of Dock Street. I felt as if I had lived and patrolled those sidewalks from childhood. It wasn't all easy, however; the night duty could be very lonely and utterly miserable at times, particularly about four a.m. on a bitterly cold winter's night when the elements were at their most foreboding, and the body was at its lowest ebb. Many a night I found myself half frozen, falling asleep, standing upright in a doorway during long night hours, with only my thoughts for company.

At such times my mind often went back to my birthplace at Horwich. It was a railway town of some 15,000 to 16,000 people, nestled under the far western slopes of the Pennine hills, which are known as the backbone of England. Apart from the Winter Hill air crash, its only claim to fame was on the second of May, 1940, when King George VI and Queen Elizabeth (now the Queen Mother) visited the locomotive works under war-time secrecy. Despite the secrecy, they were given a festive welcome by the flag-waving crowds lining their route from the railway station to the locomotive works, which were being used in the production of tanks and other war materials.

I had spent a happy childhood in Horwich. For as long as I could remember my parents had owned a general store and hardware business. It was a double-fronted shop, situated on one of the town's main thoroughfares. Over the door was my mother's name M. A. Leech. When I was about 14 years old, my friend Joan used to tease me by calling it "Ma Leech's shop." That used to make me mad!

Besides the shop, my father worked full-time at the locomotive works. Both my parents were extremely hardworking, industrious people. They were well respected in the community, and Dad's motto was to give personal satisfaction to the customer. He was proud of the fact that during all the years he and Mum had owned the store they had never run out of paraffin, even during the very severe winter of 1940 when communications with other towns were cut off. He was prepared to go to great lengths to keep his reputation of reliability to his customers intact, and his word was his bond.

I recall one especially severe winter when I was in my early teens. Dad was too wise to be caught napping, and he almost daily checked his paraffin tank and took stock of the weather and other factors which might affect the sale or delivery. He had ordered well in advance to cope with possible delays due to snow-blocked roads and excessive demand, but due to circumstances beyond his control, the scheduled delivery had not taken place. The days rolled by with a continuous drain on the fuel stock because of the inclement weather. One particular Saturday we were down to our last few gallons when Dad sent me out with instructions to go and buy paraffin from another hardware merchant at the other end of town. This dealer charged considerably more while Dad still sold it at his own original price, selling it at a loss in order not to disappoint his customers!

Father wanted me to take over the business when I left school, but he knew that the decision would have to come from me voluntarily. In order to help me make a correct decision, he involved me over the years in every aspect of the trade. My tasks included weighing out bags of plaster of Paris, cement, and whitening; delivering orders; checking shipments of goods to see that they were correctly invoiced; pricing and marking of individual items; accounting and banking details. And on Saturdays when we were busy I was even allowed the great privilege of serving behind the counter. He trained me so thoroughly that I had no false illusions about owning my own business, and I was only too ready to opt out of such a mundane way of life. When the time came for the decision to be made, the thrill and excitement of the police force easily took precedence.

Well, now I was in the police force, and here I was on a cold winter's night, thinking of home and family. I was freezing cold despite the heavy greatcoat and ponderous cape I was wearing. It was pitch black and the doorway where I was standing afforded me scant protection from the elements. My limbs were stiff and numb from the extreme cold. A biting wind was sweeping across Morecambe Bay and seemed to penetrate the very joints and marrow of my bones. I forced myself to concentrate and listened hard — not a sound, not a whisper of noise, not even the glow or glimmer of a friendly light, however small, to break up the seemingly impenetrable blackness — nothing but the solitude of the night, and dawn was still far off. I thought of my father, probably sleeping peacefully at that very moment, and of the security he had in fixed hours of employment and an undisturbed sleep every night. I smiled ruefully to myself. So much for my ideas of adventure and excitement!

Although my parents were hardworking, law-abiding citizens, they were not regular church attenders. They were affiliated with the local chapel and quietly contributed in a variety of ways to its functional roles but without any pretentious outward show.

I was encouraged to attend the various activities revolving

around the church. For over ten years I regularly attended worship and participated in a wide range of sports and pastimes which were part and parcel of the church's life. Apart from the traditional pattern of formal worship morning and evening on Sundays, with an afternoon Sunday school class in between, the church organized a Christian Endeavor program and ran a boys' brigade program known as "pilots" which enthusiastically took part in annual district Bible competitions. For the youth the highlight was the Saturday evening dances which were held in the Sunday school hall. They were climaxed by the last waltz which sometimes resulted in a mad scramble to ask the girl of your current choice to do you the honor of being your partner. Acceptance traditionally afforded one the opportunity of escorting her home immediately afterwards.

I cannot honestly recall what type of sermons were preached. I do not know whether the gospel of Christ was ever proclaimed during my decade or so of association with that church. I know now that I had no personal relationship with the Savior of mankind. I had made many friends of my own age through the church, and I suppose that was the main reason that kept me there for so long. But there were some things that, even as a small boy, I could not quite reconcile myself to. There was the time when I had walked into the sparsely attended sanctuary of the church one Sunday morning and, after having selected a completely empty pew in which to sit, I was promptly told that I couldn't sit there because it had been paid for by Mr. ... and that only he and his family were allowed to use it! This seemed a rather strange custom to me, and even at that tender age I was offended by it.

There were some amusing incidents, too. I remember one occasion especially. The organist, who was very deaf, had asked us to give him a signal when the minister had finished saying the main prayer so that he could commence playing the instrument as a lead into the singing of the Lord's Prayer. He sat behind and above the minister with his back facing the congregation and he looked into his mirror, somewhat like a car rearview mirror, to see what was happening. At the end of the minister's prayer, we duly obliged by nodding vigorously with our combined heads, and he struck up beautifully right on cue. This arrangement worked admirably for several weeks, until we decided to play a joke on him. When the minister was still in the middle of what seemed to us an interminable prayer, we all nodded our heads vigorously. Our organist began and the minister's droning words were completely drowned by the chords of the instrument, much to the consternation of the congregation. We giggled uncontrollably. I don't think he ever trusted us again!

Now I drifted back to consciousness and reality once again. The first streaks of a pale gray dawn were appearing in the sable sky, and a glance at my watch told me it was time to move on and keep my 5:00 a.m. appointment at the tram shelter telephone booth. I breathed in deeply and held my breath as I walked along until my lungs were almost bursting. This was the most effective way I knew of waking up and generating body heat, even though it was a kill or cure method.

I lengthened my stride in order not to be late and so incur the wrath of the sergeant, who might be waiting to see me in the comfort of his heated patrol car. I compared my past life with my present one. The two situations were poles apart. The quiet, respectable home background and upbringing did not appear to have any relevance whatsoever to the harsh reality of my present world.

In the two years at Fleetwood I suppose the world would say I had my mind "broadened." I gave up all semblance of being a churchgoer, along with the 99.9 percent of other policemen I knew. So far as I knew, the only ones who attended were a few Roman Catholics, and this small number only did so when it was absolutely necessary in order to put on some kind of appearance to the priestly authorities. I was finished with such conduct, and my past faded into obscurity as the world drew me uncompromisingly into its mold.

"The heart is deceitful above all things, and beyond cure. Who can understand it?" (Jeremiah 17:9, NIV).

Mixed Blessings
Chapter Three

O n the 19th of September, 1959, Joan and I were married in our hometown parish church at Horwich. We had been childhood sweethearts, and later our courtship resumed when I became a police cadet in the town.

Joan had just passed her 20th birthday five days earlier. I do not remember many details of the actual ceremony, but I can still recapture afresh my beautiful bride looking a picture of radiance in her long white dress and train.

The occasion had not been without its drama. To save expense, we had engaged our former geography teacher to take the photographs. He was a tremendous enthusiast of no small skill; but unfortunately he went to the wrong parish church in the town. There was only a short time to spare when he discovered his error. He had already taken a whole series of pictures of a completely different wedding! Finally he arrived, breathless, just in time to capture Joan as she was arriving. The marriage was delayed some minutes while he took photographs.

This incident was more than compensated for when we left the church with a guard of honor consisting of members of the St. John's Ambulance Brigade, representing Joan, and policemen with truncheons held aloft forming an archway under which we walked arm in arm as man and wife.

During our nine-month engagement we had seen very little of each other. I had hunted high and low for a flat or living accommodation of some kind in the Fleetwood area, but without success. Finally I found a middle-aged couple who were prepared to rent part of their home. This meant our accommodation was not self-contained, and Joan had to share the kitchen with the lady of the house. My inspector warned me against this course of action, saying that two women never got on together in the same kitchen, but I had little choice. How his words were to ring in my ears over the ensuing weeks.

Mrs. W. ... was kind, thoughtful and helpful in many ways, desiring nothing but the best for us. She assisted Joan in baking, planning meals, shopping, the wise spending of money and general housekeeping duties. But at the time, due to our immaturity, we did not fully appreciate her well-meant efforts, and we never felt completely at ease. Even though Mrs. W. ... sincerely wanted us to feel at home, tension was inevitably there. I know Joan felt a sense of frustration. She wished to have the freedom of a wife to learn independently how to make her husband's meals, including burnt offerings, without supervision. On reflection, we both now believe that if at all possible, young couples should start off married life on their own.

Fortunately, after a few months I was able to secure a two-roomed, self-contained flat situated on the Esplanade. Here we had a wonderful view overlooking Morecambe Bay where we could watch the Isle of Man steamers come majestically up the narrow channel. The constant stream of trawlers, both day and night, never ceased to enthrall us.

The policy of the police force during this time was to offer housing accommodation to their married men within the first nine to twelve months of marriage. In June of 1960, the inspector sent for me and told me that, although he wanted to keep me in Fleetwood itself, there were no houses currently vacant, and I was now due to be allocated the next married posting. He told me, however, that he could keep me in the division of Fleetwood by offering me a house at Thornton-Cleveleys. This was a very select seaside resort situated midway between Fleetwood and Blackpool, totally different in character and populace from our present location. Joan and I went and looked at the house, which was a large semi-detached affair, the front downstairs room being a police office. Despite this, the building was more than adequate for our needs and we gratefully accepted our first house.

But my gratitude was short-lived. I learned almost over-night to absolutely loathe the whole situation. In comparison to Fleetwood, this place was lifeless. There were no drunks or criminals to arrest. Most of the residents were wealthy middle-aged or elderly people who had bought out the original inhabitants for large sums of money in order to enjoy their years of retirement in restful, undisturbed seclusion. Many of them were extremely independent, and I found it almost impossible to develop a meaningful relationship with them.

Most of my daytime duties consisted of patrolling short sections of the promenade, insuring that cars did not infringe the parking laws. I was nothing more than a glorified car park attendant or traffic warden. My tours of duty dragged by interminably in direct contrast to Fleetwood, where the time had seemingly flown. I became very discontented and grumbled constantly to my wife. She could not fully under-stand the quite abrupt change in my attitude. I had never complained before when we lived at the fishing port, and I was at some pains to explain that I had joined the Lancashire Constabulary for excitement and adventure, not to play at being a highly paid car park attendant. (This was really sarcasm; our wage then in 1960 was in the region of seven pounds per week.) Every day became an absolute drag, and I couldn't wait to get off duty and away from the monotony of repeatedly pacing up and down alongside the double yellow lines painted in the roadway. The sergeant had firmly in-

structed me to pounce on the unsuspecting motorists who were
mainly holiday makers seeking to get the best view of the
beach and rolling sea, and who were blissfully unaware of
being in breach of the local parking regulations until brought to
a rude awakening by my appearance.

But this kind of duty could hardly be compared with what
had occurred at Fleetwood. I felt disillusioned and trapped, but
no one else seemed to be able to understand my attitude. Most
of the other men were quite content to idle their time away
doing nothing of any consequence, but there was no esprit de
corps among them and petty squabbles were frequent. I knew I
was degenerating as a policeman because there was very little
active work to do, and I felt I couldn't go on in this way.

The situation got so grave that we gave serious consideration to my resigning from the service and of emigrating to
Australia. However, just at that time we were awarded a
massive pay raise (after which we were christened "the 1,000
pound a year policemen"), and we decided to stay on a little
longer. But I knew my basic problem had not been answered.

In mid-December, 1960, five months after we had moved to
Thornton-Cleveleys, I read in our Force weekly bulletin that
volunteers were needed for a place called Kirkby. The article
stated that excellent four bedroom houses were being offered
with the posting, and that after a two-year period of service one
would be allowed to transfer at the Force's expense to more
congenial surroundings. I didn't know much about Kirkby,
other than the fact that it was a growing town which had been
built on the outskirts of the city of Liverpool, to accommodate
thousands of people being moved out of the city center because
of its slum clearance program.

I went home that night and told Joan about this most
unusual advertisement in the weekly bulletin. We decided that
on my next rest day we would go and have a quiet look around
the area and "case the joint," to use criminal jargon. This we
did. To us, the town just seemed an unending maze of brand

new housing projects with little or no shopping facilities. Hundreds of poorly clad children were roaming all over the glass-strewn streets, but my wife said she didn't see any two-headed monsters, as she had been led to believe she would. So we decided to give the place a try. After all, if we didn't like it then I could still resign and emigrate.

It was Christmas Eve, 1960, when I typed out my application to volunteer for duty at Kirkby. I was working the 2 to 10 p.m. shift, commonly referred to as "afternoons," and the application was the last thing I did before I finished duty that evening. I handed it to the duty sergeant for his perusal and signature so that it could be forwarded to divisional headquarters (D.H.Q.). His eyes bulged like organ stops when he read the report. He stared incredulously first at the report, then at me, and he seemed to be speechless. When he finally regained his composure, he asked me if I really knew what I was doing. It was a fair question, because I hadn't discussed the matter with anyone else, and I *didn't* know what I was doing. All I knew was that any other place would be preferable. When he saw my mind was made up, he signed the application and put it in the correspondence bag which was awaiting collection for dispatch to D.H.Q.

I rode home on my bicycle that night as if I had wings. There was a song in my heart and renewed hope in the police force, as I contemplated the exciting adventures that would undoubtedly lie before us at Kirkby if my application was accepted.

I could hardly restrain my impatience as I waited for the reply but was overjoyed when I received an affirmative answer. There was one alteration in the terms however — the four bedroom house originally referred to had been withdrawn by the police authority and instead a three bedroom house in another area was offered. The report suggested I might like to go and look over the house before making a final decision. This we decided to do.

Many months later I learned why the other houses were no longer available. One of the assistant chief constables, apparently very disturbed that men were refusing to move into these particular houses in Kirkby, went to inspect them. He had gone in a chauffeur-driven, highly polished black Jaguar which was left parked outside while he and the police driver examined the empty house. The assistant chief constable apparently was extremely impressed with the houses and said there was no reason why men should refuse to move into them. He would ensure that they were occupied immediately!

But then he looked out of the front window and was horrified to see hordes of young children swarming all over his gleaming new automobile. They were even scampering over the roof, causing scratch marks and minor indentations on its resplendent bodywork. He immediately exclaimed that no men of his were going to be forced to live under such conditions, and he ordered the two houses to be disposed of forthwith!

Knowing nothing of this, Joan and I went to inspect the three-bedroom house. After considerable difficulty we finally found the police station to pick up the key to the house. The station was merely a single story, temporary wooden structure with only one brick cell, which I later learned was totally inadequate. We had been travelling for some time, so when I was handed the key I asked where my wife and I could buy a cup of tea or coffee. The station duty constable grinned cheerfully and told me there wasn't a place in town. He invited us into the refreshment room, where he gave us a very welcome cup of strong tea. I don't think we would have been so quick to accept the tea if we had known then what I later saw with my own eyes. During the night watches, it was a common sight to see mice scurrying across the kitchen sink, only to disappear with uncanny speed in all directions when any would-be captor approached.

Joan and I inspected the house and were extremely pleased. We decided to accept the transfer and moved into our

second police house in February, 1961. Joan was now two
months pregnant.

Kirkby New Town

Chapter Four

During two and one half years on the police force I thought I had learned how to swear-or at least had heard all the profane language there was to know. How wrong I was! Even some of the women swore better than any horse trooper or company sergeant major.

We had been living in the district only a few days when my wife got her first taste of such conduct. We were returning home on foot from a shopping trip. As we passed a three-story apartment building a window on the third story was suddenly thrust open, and a woman in her mid-thirties leaned out and literally screamed a torrent of abuse and obscenities at a little girl, only three or four years old, playing on a tiny plot of ground below. I felt myself blushing, especially since Joan was with me, but I didn't know how to deal with the situation. We kept on walking as if nothing had happened, but I resolved that I was going to protect my wife from this as much as possible.

We hit upon a plan. We began visiting the shops as soon as they opened in the morning, before most people were stirring. Thus we had them virtually to ourselves and were able to make our purchases quickly and be back home before the town had really awakened.

There was surprisingly little drunkenness in Kirkby for the size of the town. But the town had more than its share of violence. This was not confined to rival gangs or warring factions but was expressed against the members of the police force, especially when the odds were heavily in favor of lawlessness. These were the days when the only means of contact for the foot or bicycle patrolmen was the public telephone. There was no such thing as a personal radio and direct contact with Headquarters. Since most of us patrolled alone, often there were awkward situations involving gangs of rowdies just spoiling for "sport" and trouble. When no phone was nearby we were left to our own ingenuity in outwitting the gangs.

To supplement the foot and bicycle patrolmen we had one area patrol car, one police van (commonly called the "Black Maria"), a dog van, and a crime patrol car which was responsible for a wider area than Kirkby itself. So we didn't always have its comforting presence.

There were many instances of out and out violence, and often the patrolmen, even though heavily outnumbered, were called into action to keep the Queen's peace. To draw one's truncheon was considered the last resort, and a comprehensive report of the circumstances had to be submitted every time it was used.

The spirit of violence against the police spilled over even to the children. Woe betide your child if the other kids discovered he was a copper's son! One policeman's little boy, only 4 or 5 years old, was deliberately pushed down a steep hill on his small tricycle by a group of other children — apparently just because his dad was a copper. The boy was unable to control the tricycle and had a nasty fall in which his face was badly disfigured.

After four months at Kirkby we moved in June, 1961, to a new police station which had been built in the town center. Of the three public services — fire brigade, ambulance, and police — we were the last in line for a public building. The other two services had been provided with new quarters for some considerable time.

There was only one occasion while I was in uniform that I failed to make an arrest after informing the person that I intended to do so. That was on St. Patrick's night. I was the area car observer that night, and we got a call on the radio to go to the scene of a domestic dispute. When we arrived the occupant of the house, a middle-aged man, requested us to eject his two sons. They were drunk and had crashed a party he was having with friends and were causing a nuisance. We told him to ask them to leave in our presence. They did so and we allowed them to go their way, making allowances for the fact that it was St. Patrick's night and half the town was celebrating.

A few minutes later, however, we were called back again to the same house. This time the two sons refused to leave, and we had to eject them forcibly. They continued their disorderly behavior outside, so we decided we would have to arrest them. When we told them we were arresting them for being drunk and disorderly they struggled against us, but we each held one of them and with little difficulty were putting them into the car.

Suddenly six women came charging out of the house, screaming abuse and setting on us, three women to each man. We found ourselves fighting a losing battle. My helmet was knocked off and kicked into the gutter. My whistle and chain were ripped from my greatcoat and I was dragged to the sidewalk, kicked, scratched, and clawed. My colleague fared no better. We were both left breathless, stretched out on the pavement, while the two men bolted up the road and the women ran back into the house and slammed the door.

I retrieved my helmet but couldn't find my whistle and chain anywhere. We got back into the police car and considered our next course of action. We hesitated to call for reinforcements just to lock up a party of screaming, drunken women, and since we knew the identity of the two men we decided to leave the matter for the night and proceed against them by summons.

The following year, again on St. Patrick's night, a terrific fight developed outside one of the Roman Catholic licensed clubs. There were only five men on duty that night — one asthmatic inspector, one sergeant due for retirement, and three comparatively junior constables. The inspector took one look at the mass of sprawling bodies and gave instructions to go and fetch "the Father."

He held his men back until the priest arrived and, although there were well over 100 men fighting and brawling all over the road, that one solitary priest sorted them all out quicker than you could say "Jack Robinson" without even lifting a finger against them. Peace was restored immediately!

The area of Kirkby itself was quite pleasant to the eye, with many new apartments and houses. There were no depressed industries areas, slum quarters or bomb craters and the atmosphere was clean and unpolluted. But many recently built properties, with all the modern amenities of bathrooms and inside toilets were reduced prematurely to slums because of improper use by the inhabitants.

Several instances of coal actually being stored in the bathtub were reported, and some residents even chopped up the inside doors for firewood. Others didn't have any floor coverings of any kind, and the only respectable piece of furniture in the place would be a large console television. It was common practice to steal garden gates and doors for burning on bonfire night, and the malicious damage caused to property in general ran into many thousands of pounds, even in the early 1960's.

Cleanliness was not held in very high esteem, and many of the houses we went into were flea ridden and stank of dirt and filth. Some occupants tried to kill the smell by pouring disinfectant all over the place, but made no effort to clear up the mess they lived in.

Although an English policeman almost never says no to a cup of tea, there was one occasion when a colleague of mine

politely refused when tea was offered to him in a jam jar. I
don't think it was so much the receptacle itself that caused him
to decline but rather the filthy state of the jar. Many is the time I
have itched uncontrollably after being in some of these dwell-
ings, and I just could not understand how people could voluntarily live in such conditions.

But it was the children I really felt sorry for. What chance
did they have in life, being brought up and raised in such
circumstances? Mum and Dad spent most of the social security
unemployment money and family allowance on beer, cigarettes
and gambling. On more than one occasion, the children caught
stealing sweets from the chain stores said they had been told to
do it by their parents who had refused them sweet money and
told them to pinch the toffees instead.

There were not many dull moments in Kirkby and, despite
the totally different culture from my own, I thoroughly enjoyed
my police work. I don't think my wife heard me grumble once
during our stay there! One dark night, precisely at midnight, I
arrested a man stealing a gate in the area of the Northwood
project.

Around 3:00 a.m. the same night I was checking out the
locked Quarry Bank Tenants Association building in total
darkness. I silently tried the door, which proved secure and felt
the windows with my hand as I walked along the front of the
building, checking to be sure none were broken or unlatched. I
completed my examination of the front without incident. But
on turning the corner I literally collided with two moving
objects.

I yelled and switched on my flashlight. Two young men
ran off in different directions like frightened rabbits. They had
just broken into the club from the rear and were in the process
of carrying off their booty — cash, cigarettes, cigars, wines and
whiskey — in a cardboard box. I was determined to get one of
them, and I succeeded in running him down. He turned out to
be the right one, for he was a runaway from an approved

school and had been loose for several days. From this youth we learned the identity of his accomplice, and he was soon arrested much to the shock of his parents, who insisted he had been home in bed.

This was my life in Kirkby New Town.

Criminal Investigation Department

Chapter Five

In May, 1962 — fifteen months after being posted to Kirkby,
I was accepted into the Criminal Investigation Department.
The first six months were a probationary period, and my
appointment was subject to ratification at the end of that time.

I was absolutely thrilled. Just twenty-two years and eleven
months old, and I was a plainclothes detective! Why, I must be
one of the youngest in the whole county! Was I proud!

I had applied for the department knowing full well that if I
accepted I would forfeit my right to leave the area after the
two-year period was over. But here was an unprecedented
opportunity to further my career, and I cheerfully waived my
rights for the privilege of being a Lancashire Constabulary
Detective.

Daily routine was to report at the office at 9:00 a.m. At 1:00
p.m., on paper at least, we then took an extended lunch break
until 3:00. Then we worked through until 5:00. Following a
further two-hour "paper" break for tea, we resumed duty at
7:00 p.m. and worked until 9:00. when we could officially finish
duty for the day. It was extremely rare, however, for anyone to
leave at 9:00, because from 9:00 onwards until the public
houses closed at 10:30 it was considered a detective's task to
circulate among the criminal fraternity at the public drinking
establishments. That way a detective got to know by sight the

habitual law breakers and which of them were spending large amounts of money. We also needed to establish which criminals were now associating with each other. New teams were constantly being formed, and it was important to keep abreast of current events and to cultivate good "informants" so that the latest rumors circulating in the underworld could be gleaned and assessed.

Sometimes we learned of a planned crime before it had been committed, so that the thieves could be caught red-handed. Much emphasis was placed on this particular aspect of a detective's work. I learned that one was only as good as the number of contacts he had. The more people one knew from the broad spectrum of society at large, the more he could ascertain useful information when investigating the wide variety of crimes which occurred in the different districts of the town. Over the years some of the men in the department developed many contacts, and through these they knew virtually everything that was going on in all quarters of the community, from the highest to the lowest levels. It astounded me how much knowledge of people and their habits was known in that one comparatively small office!

Due to work pressures, there were many times when we did not take our full time off during the lunch and tea breaks. Before our day off each week we were allowed an "early finish" at 6:00 p.m. We had one full weekend off in every seven weeks, so being a member of the Criminal Investigation Department now became a vocation instead of a job. I discovered that the loyalty and dedication of the vast majority of these men were second to none.

While certain fixed allowances were paid to compensate for the extra hours performed and plain clothes now worn, no paid overtime was permitted. The allowances never really covered the actual number of hours of duty performed and, consequently, we worked many hours each week with neither payment nor time off. All this extra duty was quietly born purely for the privilege of being counted a "jack" (or detective). Most weeks we would work anywhere from sixty to eighty hours on duty, and it was common to exceed these figures when work demanded it.

Almost without exception, every member of the C.I.D. throughout the whole of the county was a drinker. In the twelve years I was on the department I can count on one hand the number of men who did not imbibe alcohol. Not to do so was to go against the accepted system and, when prospective candidates were interviewed for their suitability for appointment to the branch, the powers that be invariably made sure that the candidates were prepared to frequent public houses and consume alcoholic beverages.

During my time at Kirkby, however, one man was appointed to the department who was a teetotaler. Rumor had it that he was a Methodist lay preacher, but I never heard him openly declare his convictions — even though he lived next door to me. He was an extremely zealous police officer and had been appointed to the C.I.D. because of the many arrests he had personally made over a period of many months.

My sergeant took exception to the fact that he was a nondrinker, and he determined to alter this state of affairs as soon as possible. One evening during his first week on duty, he accompanied the sergeant and me on our rounds of the public houses; when asked what he would like to drink, he asked for a nonalcoholic beverage. The sergeant promptly told him this was not acceptable in the department, and when he saw him wavering in his conviction he immediately insisted that he have a glass of beer. For the remainder of the night, he plied this man with alcoholic drinks until he became quite drunk. Later that night it was a very sorry looking lay-preacher who was propped up against his own front door by two snickering detectives, who bolted like naughty school children when his wife opened the door in response to their knocking.

I think the sergeant was then satisfied that, despite this

man's so-called religious convictions, he was just another ordinary person who had succumbed to the temptations of the world. The poor man never really settled to the way of life expected of a C.I.D. officer, and he did not last very long on the branch. Everyone, without exception, was expected to conform to the system, and hard drinkers who could hold their liquor were looked upon with high esteem.

I had been in the department for only a few months when a series of factory break-ins took place on the Kirkby Industrial Trading Estate. A wide variety of goods were being stolen. The items ranged from furniture and office equipment, including tables, chairs, typewriters and filing cabinets, right down to pots, pans and even a kettle used for brewing tea. I was given the job of investigating the latest burglary, which was the sixth committed during a three-week period.

An examination of the scene proved unfruitful, but on making inquiries at the factories in the surrounding area, I came across a small shed which housed a one-man metal-working and welding business. The owner said that the previous afternoon he had seen several boys in their early teens hanging around the attacked premises for a considerable period of time and for no apparent reason. He said he would not be able to recognize any of them, and the only description he could give me, apart from their approximate ages, was that they were accompanied by a distinctive looking mongrel dog which he would be able to identify immediately. When I asked him to describe the animal, he said he wasn't very good at using words but he could draw a picture for me much better. He then proceeded to sketch for me a very fine picture of a large, bushy-tailed dog.

I felt the excitement rising in my blood. I believed I would be able to recognize the animal if I saw it, but where to start looking? There were literally hundreds of dogs roaming the town, and I had no guarantee of finding one among so many. However, since that was the only clue I had to work on, I selected as a starting point the nearest estate to this particular group of factories. For two days I combed the streets, sketch in hand, searching for my bushy-tailed dog, but without success. My enthusiasm was beginning to wane, but I was determined to make sure I had systematically covered everyplace I could think of.

Suddenly, shortly before teatime on the afternoon of the second day, I spotted the dog scampering across one of the grassy areas adjacent to a block of high flats. There was no mistaking it. There just couldn't be two dogs identical to the sketch I had before me. I studied the dog without approaching too closely. Just as I thought! No collar or owner's name tag on it. It could be hours before it returned to its home and master.

Just then a group of young children walked past. I spoke to them, and pointing out the dog, I asked them if they knew who the mongrel dog belonged to. One of the children readily supplied me with a full name and address.

My diligence had been rewarded so far. I went to the address given me and knocked on the door. The door opened and a youth stood before me. I produced my warrant card, told him who I was and said, "I am investigating a series of factory break-ins which have taken place on the Kirkby Industrial Estate in recent weeks, and I have reason to believe that you are one of the persons responsible. What have you to say about these matters?"

My direct approach paid off. He immediately replied, "I'm sorry, sir. We've looked after everything we've took and it's all safe."

I was flabbergasted but tried not to show it. It was one of the easiest confessions I had ever gotten. He accompanied me in the C.I.D. car back to the estate where he took me to an unoccupied factory. Inside was every single item of stolen property from all of the six factories burglarized. Several youngsters had been involved, and they imagined themselves as factory owners and workers and had set up a make-believe business by stealing everything needed to run a factory, even down to the materials required for brewing tea!

The aggrieved factory owners were delighted to have their stolen equipment returned undamaged and intact, and I made particular friends with one of the owners and his wife, who sought to express their gratitude in a number of unexpected ways.

My new friend asked me one day if I had thought of joining a Masonic lodge, to which I truthfully replied in the negative. My knowledge about the organization was very limited, and most of what I had heard was folklore and rumor rather than firsthand information. My friend told of the charitable works the Masonic fraternity participated in, and he said that in addition to helping other people, membership could also help one's career, since many high-ranking police officers were Masons. After thinking the matter over, I decided no harm could come from such a venture. So my friend introduced me to a man who later proposed me to his lodge which was in the Liverpool city center.

After scrutiny and various interviews, I was accepted as a lodge member and passed through the three initiation ceremonies to become a Master Mason. I must say that I never at any time felt a real affinity or sense of dedication to the Masonic cause, despite the warmth and friendship extended to me, especially my proposer. The idea of "helping my career along" was merely an illusive dream. There were no Lancashire Constabulary officers in this particular lodge, and during the five years I was a Mason I attended only one function in which other members of my police force were present. Besides, I had always determined I would get promoted by hard work and dedication and scorned the saying that, "It's not what you know but who you know that counts." I was determined to advance on job merit and not by hobnobbing with the brass. And, I never saw the necessity or relevance of what took place in the actual Masonic ceremonies despite all the pomp, solemnity and ornate uniform.

A large proportion of reported crime in Kirkby was committed by juveniles. Consequently, I spent a considerable amount of time giving evidence before the juvenile panel of magistrates. I remember well one small, insignificant looking schoolboy of some eleven or twelve years of age whom I dealt with for varied offenses of burglary. He was making his fourth or fifth appearance before the bench, and when the magistrates retired from the courtroom to make a decision as to what to do with him he said to me, "You know, Mr. Leech, the magistrates are bloody liars."

His tone off voice was so emphatic that I asked him why he said that. He then told me of his past court experiences. He said that at every court appearance the chairman had solemnly warned him that this was his "last chance," but they always gave him another one. So it was a rather stunned boy a few minutes later who found himself being separated from his parents and sent to a detention center. This time the magistrates had kept their word, but it taught me the importance of meaning what I said, even to young children! Once I have threatened punishment for future misbehavior to my own children, I have always carried out my threat if they subsequently disobeyed. I have found that, provided they have been warned previously and know that their actions are wrong, they accept punishment without bitterness or resentment and a right and meaningful relationship is fostered between parent and child.

Things went well for me in the department. I had two very capable detective sergeants who took my training very seriously, and I had a number of experienced colleagues to whom I could always turn for advice. Due to the great number of criminal offenses perpetrated in this notorious town, I learned much from first-hand experience. This thorough groundwork learned during my time at Kirkby was to stand me in good stead in later years.

Maghull
Chapter Six

O n the 23rd of December, 1963, just under three years after moving to Kirkby, I was offered a transfer to the nearby township of Maghull. Although only a few miles away, Maghull was entirely different from Kirkby. It was considered the next step in the promotion stakes, as there was only one other detective stationed at this considerably smaller and well-respected town. Here the challenge would be to put into practice what I had already learned, without having the sergeant's arm to lean upon. I knew that if I made a success of this posting, then, provided the examinations were passed, promotion would not be far away. So I gladly accepted the transfer, even though it meant moving the day before Christmas Eve, and Joan was almost eight months pregnant with our second child.

I reported for duty on Christmas morning. We had had only two days to settle into our new home. During that short span of time we discovered a wiring fault in the electrical system which affected the electric cooker and all the house lights. We were faced with the prospect of cold meals and candlelight for Christmas, but fortunately this was averted through the Electricity Board authorities, who gave us a temporary connection to see us through the holiday period. Happy in the knowledge that my expectant wife and young son were able to partake of warm food and drink, I faced up to my new challenge.

At Kirkby, the whole town had been a hive of activity with people hustling and bustling everywhere, the telephone constantly ringing, an office full of colleagues for company, and a seemingly endless list of crimes to deal with. Here at Maghull the pace was quite leisurely. Some days no crimes were reported at all. The telephone remained silent most of the time. I often had the office to myself with just the four walls to stare at, since my solitary colleague was frequently engaged in duties elsewhere or had the day off. Even the bosses from Division at Headquarters seemed to treat me differently now that I was no longer at Kirkby, and I found myself in a completely new world. There were not as many crimes to report, but I had a far wider area to cover including Aintree, home of the Grand National Racecourse, and several small villages.

I found I was able to spend more time investigating each individual crime, but the offenses were usually harder to detect because many of the thieves, especially the burglars, were traveling criminals. Very few serious lawbreakers actually lived on my "patch," but it was considered fair game for the city teams who raided the better class houses and farms with almost monotonous regularity. We would no sooner get one gang behind bars then another one would spring up.

I recall one of my first visits to the Hare and Hounds pub at Maghull. I wanted to make contacts and establish relationships with people who would be of assistance to me in my war against crime. This particular pub was very lively and busy and attracted people from several miles around. Active criminals were said to patronize the place unknown to the landlord.

I made acquaintance with a chap at the bar, and we had a few drinks together. He seemed like an extremely useful contact, since he knew much of what was going on in the district. He was quite willing to talk, and I recalled one of my former detective sergeant's words when I was first posted to the department at Kirkby: "When you have established a relationship with someone, make sure he remembers your name so that when he has any useful information he will ring the Station and ask for you personally. That way you will get the information and the credit when it proves good."

That particular sergeant's name was Phillips, and there was a nationally known firm by the same name which manufactured rubber soles and heels for shoes. So in order to impress his name upon the person's mind he would say. "My name's Phillips. Think of soles and heels for shoes, and you can't forget it." This way, he said, he impressed his name upon the minds of newfound contacts and thereby benefited by receiving information directly from them and not second hand.

I had not forgotten this piece of valuable advice, so now on my new patch I tried to think of a way by which my contact would not forget my name. I said to him, "My name is Leech, spelled L-E-E-C-H, the same as a bloodsucker." (Most people in England spell it Leach.) "Think of a bloodsucker, and you can't forget it." With these parting words I left my newfound contact, wondering whether his promise to let me know what he found out among his underworld friends was sincere or not.

A few days later, a very puzzled station duty constable approached me and said, "There's been some kind of a nut on the telephone, asking for the C.I.D. I asked him who he wanted to speak to and he told me, 'Mr. Bloodsucker.' I said we didn't have anyone by that name in the department, but he insisted there was and hung up angrily when I insisted there wasn't."

I didn't know whether to laugh or weep! Here was my first piece of information coming in on my new patch from my very first contact, only to be turned away on the telephone by one of my uniformed colleagues! But, I was able to make contact with the man afterwards and rectify the situation.

There were 27 pubs, or public houses, on my patch and I religiously visited them all regularly, building up a network of contacts. I was tempted to frequent the better class of pub rather than the rougher ones, but it was the road houses and rougher pubs where most of the useful information was obtained, so I called on them all.

One night while making the rounds in the public houses I received a tip-off that dangerous drugs were being held in a house at Melling. My contact was a reliable one, and the information he supplied was quite comprehensive, so the following day I obtained a magistrates' search warrant. We decided to arrive at the house just after tea time to try and catch our suspect at home before he went out for the evening. We parked our vehicle some distance from the house and approached on foot. Two men covered the rear, and one other colleague and myself went to the front door. Armed with the warrant, I knocked on the door, which had been amateurishly painted bright purple. It was opened by an attractive but untidily dressed young woman. I explained who we were, and after I read the warrant to her she let us into the house, informing us that her "husband" had not returned home for his tea.

We began searching the house. My lot fell to examining the kitchen, one corner of which was under the stairs. I started to lift out all the accumulated junk from the corner. I found all kinds of miscellaneous rubbish, including a vacuum cleaner which I proceeded to dismantle. Opening the inside, I saw a paper bag and started to pull it out. The young woman insisted it was part of the cleaner, but as I pulled it out the bottom burst and a round tin fell at my feet. I thought that I had "struck oil," but when I opened it I gasped with surprise when I saw that it contained a stick of explosive! Examining the rest of the bag's contents I found another similar tin, this one containing a number of detonators! In addition, there was also a high-powered electrical battery, wire for connecting the charge, and putty to be used as tamping material. There was everything, in fact, to make up a complete safe-blowing kit! We sat in the house until the early hours of the morning, when the male occupant eventually returned, obviously under the influence of drugs. Although we found no drugs, either in his home or on his person, we arrested him for unlawful possession of explosives. He was later sentenced to four years imprisonment.

While I was stationed at Maghull, a divisional night duty detective rotation system was introduced. With this system, every three months or so it came my turn to perform full night duty for a week, covering not only Maghull itself, but the whole Seaforth division. This method was employed so that all the other detectives could get a night of undisturbed sleep without being knocked out of bed to deal with prisoners arrested during the night.

About 3:00 a.m. on the 10th of June, 1965, I was working the night duty, and we had been extremely busy. I was just sitting down to a very belated supper in the refreshment room at Crosby Police Station when the station duty constable rushed in and said I was wanted on the phone by the night sergeant at Divisional Headquarters. It was urgent.

I immediately went to the switchboard and the sergeant told me to leave everything and get over to Seaforth with all possible speed. He wasn't prepared to disclose what the circumstances were even over the internal police telephone network, so I knew it must be something serious. I rounded up the two "Z" car men with whom I patrolled the division and we headed at top speed for the D.H.Q. We were there within minutes. The sergeant looked very relieved to see me. He told me a teleprinter message had been received from the Staffordshire County Police stating that a woman had been murdered a few hours earlier, and a man who lived in our area was wanted for interview in connection with the crime. He was to be arrested and detained on their behalf.

I quickly asked him how many men he could spare me and he said, "Three." I thought that was plenty since I already had two men with me, so, having obtained the necessary details from the sergeant, we headed for the address given us, which was a flat above a grocery shop.

We approached quietly and parked our vehicles some distance from the shop and moved in on foot. The place was in darkness. The flat could be entered only through the rear yard gate and up a wooden flight of stairs. The gate latch responded to our touch, and we slowly pushed the gate open. We entered the yard, climbed the stairs and tried the door, but it was locked. There were no signs of life. We had already done a rough calculation of the time and had decided that it was unlikely he could have arrived home so quickly because of the distance involved between the two towns. So we merged into the darkness and surrounded the premises, keeping well out of sight.

We had not taken up our positions for more than ten minutes when we heard footsteps coming along the cobbled street. A figure passed close by my colleague and me. We waited with bated breath as we saw him open the yard gate and start to climb the stairs. We moved silently after him and crept stealthily up the stairs. I sensed my companion easing his truncheon out of its pocket in case our man should turn violent.

The suspect switched on his living room light and was just putting the kettle under the cold water tap when he saw us standing unannounced in his doorway. I must say he was a very cool customer. We had caught him completely off guard, and yet his composure never gave way. He offered no resistance but insisted he had no idea whatsoever as to why we had visited him at that unearthly hour. When we arrived back at the station with the suspect, the sergeant said to me, "Good work, Ken. Did you get the gun?"

"Gun! What gun?" I said.

"Oh," he said, "he killed her with a repeater shotgun, didn't I tell you? Sorry. I thought I had.

"The murder had apparently been motivated by jealousy and revenge. The woman with whom he had been living had left him to marry another man. He said he would take his revenge on them both, and his hatred had obviously festered until he had turned his evil thoughts into concrete actions. But his plan backfired on him, for in his haste he shot the wrong woman. His victim was not his former mistress, but an innocent member of her husband's family.

Throughout the whole trial at Worcestershire Assize Court, the man pleaded his innocence, but the jury unanimously found him guilty of murder. It was a moment of extreme solemnity when the black cap was placed on the judge's head, and he pronounced the sentence of death. Capital punishment was still in force in the country at that time, and this man was one of the very last to be sentenced to death by hanging. However, he was subsequently reprieved by the Home Secretary, and the death penalty was soon after abolished.

We never did find the murder weapon. I smile to myself now as I think about it. The English "bobby" is totally unarmed except for his wooden truncheon, and every year a number of them gallantly forfeit their lives as they tackle desperate armed criminals. The price paid to maintain public sympathy and support is far from a cheap one.

South West Crime Squad

Chapter Seven

During the second half of 1967 I was transferred from Maghull to what was then known as the South West Crime Squad. The transfer resulted from a chance meeting with one of the chief inspectors in that unit. I was doing my round of the public houses one night and went into one of my regular haunts in Lydiate. Standing at the bar was the chief inspector, I had heard he had just moved into the area, although the Crime Squad office itself was based at my old stamping ground of Kirkby. We knew each other by sight but had never worked together, so I was a little on the defensive at first when he started to talk to me. I thawed out somewhat after a few beers, and we had quite a congenial conversation together. After a while he asked me how long I had been in the detective department, and I said, "Five years." He then asked me if I had thought of going into the crime squad. Now not every one took kindly to the squad, and I had been one of its critics. They seemed always to be driving around in big cars and were always busy on some important case if someone asked for assistance at any time. So I replied, "No, I haven't."

"Think it over," he said, and I told him I would.

I suppose I was a little flattered to think that he would consider me a suitable candidate for the squad. I talked it over with Joan, and she said if that was what I wanted to do, then it was all right with her. I was beginning to feel I was in a rut, and perhaps this was just what my career needed. I knew, however, that I would have to pass the police examinations to stand any chance of promotion. I had already failed them on three occasions. I wasn't spending sufficient time preparing for them, and I knew it.

But after a couple of interviews I found myself transferred to the crime squad. I was based at its headquarters in Kirkby, but I was permitted to continue living in Maghull, which pleased my family.

There were two chief inspectors on this squad. One had the reputation of being a "tartar" but was commonly referred to as "laughing Jack!" He had been one of the two headquarters hatchet men with the job of investigating complaints against the police, and he was held in awe by every one I knew. He was reputedly one of the best murder investigators in the force. He was renowned for his unique aptitude for interrogation, coupled with a keen analytical brain and a sixth sense about human nature. He was extremely shrewd, and even seasoned C.I.D. men knew they couldn't pull the wool over his eyes. He had a dark, swarthy complexion; piercing, deep set eyes; and a dour disposition. He was broad shouldered and had the constitution of an ox! He looked as though his face would crack if he actually smiled, and I suppose that is how he got the nickname, "laughing Jack." As far as I could see, he only had one weakness, and that was drink.

In the following months I came to learn much about this man, and I found my admiration for him growing daily. He stressed loyalty and said that it was a two-way action. If a boss wanted loyalty from his men, then he had to be loyal to them. He certainly proved his loyalty for me on many occasions over the next few years. In the end I would willingly have laid my life down for him.

During my early months on the squad, he insisted that I do as much studying as possible for the promotion examinations.

On many occasions he deliberately sent me home early in order to do just that. I suppose I was fearful of what would happen if I failed them this time after all his help, so I made a really determined assault on the studies. I took the examinations in January of 1968, and to my great delight, I passed them with flying colors. By virtue of my high marks I qualified for consideration for the Police College at Bramshill. After a year at Police College, promotion to sergeant was automatic, and after serving an additional year on operational police duties one would be made an inspector.

This was certainly a rapid way of promotion, but there were many pitfalls along the road. First off, the candidate had to satisfy his own local force of his suitability before being allowed to make the trip to London for the next stage in the process. I was one of about seventeen from Lancashire who was permitted the trip south to London. There, a panel of distinguished senior police officials, civil servants and former military men conducted a series of half-hour interviews by which they reduced the 360 candidates to 36!

I remember the interview well. I was taken into a room and given a seat in front of four men who were busily scribbling notes on pads of paper. Apparently they were compiling their impressions of the previous applicant. The interview began quietly enough, but soon came very searching questions about a number of subjects. I wasn't worried, because I really didn't think I had any chance of being accepted. At 28, I was probably too old. I had been too long in the service; they were looking for men with only three or four years of service. Reportedly they didn't like criminal investigation officers, or people with northern accents. I was a loser on all counts! Since I had nothing going for me, I gave it all I had and refused to let them browbeat me.

I was asked to comment about any relevant news item of public interest outside of police work, and I chose the subject of Rhodesia. When asked why. I replied that it was not every year that a country committed treason and was allowed to get away with it! This seemed to go down quite well with one of the panel members, who I subsequently learned had been a British Army Officer in Rhodesia some years previously.

The questions continued until the allotted half-hour had elapsed. Before I had time to rise from my seat and without even the courtesy of bidding me so much as a "good morning." These four men had their heads bowed low over the table and were writing furiously on their pieces of paper, leaving me still sitting in the chair. I saw red! I stood up, and inhaling a goodly supply of air, I spoke as authoritatively as I could, with a hint of sarcasm in my voice.

"Gentlemen!" Their heads shot bolt upright. "Good morning." And I abruptly turned and marched briskly out of the room, not waiting to note their response to my outburst. Ah well, I thought, it has been a day out and a change from routine but that's the end of that.

But in fact it was not all over. A few weeks later word came through that I was one of the successful 36 candidates, and that I had now qualified for the final selection board. Only one other man from Lancashire had survived the grilling. I learned that these 36 men would be divided into two groups of 18, each of which would attend a three-day extended series of interviews at Eastbourne on the south coast of England. There were all kinds of rumors circulating about the nature of this obstacle course. It apparently ranged from intelligence tests, English composition, and general knowledge subjects to conducting meetings during which you were to play the part of chairman and a series of private and group interviews with members of the selection committee. I was the last of the 18 candidates to have my interview with the full panel. I made sure I was there in good time. When I had been shown into the room and given a seat, the chairman said, "You've enjoyed these three days, haven't you, Leech."

"Yes Sir," I replied.

"Why is that?" he asked.

"I think it is because I like competition. I can only give of my best and that is what I have done here. If it is not good enough, then there is nothing more I can do about it."

I was then closely questioned regarding my years on the C.I.D. and as to where my aspirations lay in the future. I rather foolishly stuck out for remaining in the department, for it wasn't this type of man they were looking for. They wanted administrators who could eventually tab command of senior posts.

Despite my obvious enthusiasm, somehow I don't think I fitted their description of a budding chief constable! I well remember one of the last questions asked of me: "Tell me, Leech, what do you know about music and the arts?"

I looked the questioner right in the eye and replied, "Nothing whatsoever, Sir. But if you consider that is the way to get to the top of the police force, then I am perfectly prepared to study those subjects at the police college for the next 12 months."

It came as no real surprise to me when I later received a form letter telling me I had not been selected for the College. Of the 18 men in my group, 11 had been C.I.D. men, and not one of them had been successful.

Whatever the panel of experts at Eastbourne might have thought of me, the Lancashire Constabulary was apparently extremely pleased I had gotten as far as I did. I was promptly promoted to Detective Sergeant, and I was to stay at Kirkby on Crime squad duties.

While I was at Kirkby, the title of the Squad was changed from the South West Crime Squad to the No. 3 District Task Force. Our department at that time consisted of only two offices on the top story of the station. They had once been designated as the library and special constables' rooms by some ambitious civil architect. We had no sooner moved out of the wooden shack laughingly referred to as a police station back in 1961 when it was decided that structural alterations would have to be made in the new building because it was found to be inadequate for its job. We needed more room because our outfit was to be expanded. No one could really believe his ears when it was first rumored that we were moving to Knowsley Hall!

Knowsley Hall belonged (and still does) to Lord Edward John Stanley, the 18th Earl of Derby, and it has been the ancestral home of the Stanley family since 1385. The title had been conferred shortly after the battle of Bosworth Field in 1485 by King Henry VII. There had been many illustrious Earls of Derby in the bygone centuries. James, the 7th Earl (1606-1651), known as the "Martyr Earl," declared his allegiance for the King at the outbreak of civil war and was proclaimed a traitor by parliament. He fought on the royalist side throughout the war, but following the battle of Worcester, he was captured and on the 15th of October, 1651, he was executed at Bolton in Lancashire. Edward Geoffrey, the 14th Earl (1799-1869) was an English statesman, leader of the Conservative party from 1846 to 1868, three times Prime Minister of England and one of the country's greatest parliamentary orators. In 1833, while Secretary of State for War and the Colonies, he introduced and carried the act of abolishing slavery in the British Empire.

The present Lord Derby was then Lord Lieutenant of Lancashire, and in 1961 he had been made a Freeman of the City of Manchester. How could his home possibly become the Headquarters of the No. 3 District Task Force?

We later learned that in 1966 Lord Derby had moved into a new house on his estate, and that he had rented one wing of the Hall to the Lancashire Police authorities. It was with considerable awe and amazement that I found myself working from the ancestral home of the Earls of Derby!

One enters the house itself by means of a fine stone stairway and through a porch added by the present Earl. This impressive historic building contains libraries, drawing rooms,

and a Jacobean room in which was a portrait of the martyred
7th Earl. In front of the fireplace is a grim memento — the very
chair on which he kneeled when he was beheaded! Although
all the details of the rooms have been many times altered, their
size and general disposition, except for the great dining room,
probably remain unchanged.

The gardens on the estate consist chiefly of wide lawns and
beautiful groups of trees. These are enclosed on the east and
south sides by a series of lakes on which a variety of geese and
ducks are often seen. It is indeed a scene perfect in its harmony
and repose, and at complete contrast with the grim occupation
of its present inhabitants whose onerous task is manhunting
among the criminal underworld of felons ranging from high
class confidence tricksters and drug pushers to vicious thugs
and homicidal maniacs.

A Murder and a Witness
Chapter Eight

Sin knows no bounds. We investigated some extremely bizarre killings — from battered babies found dead in their own cots, to teenagers of both sexes murdered for sexual gratification or perversion, right through the age range to our senior citizens. I vividly recall the case of an 80-year-old widow who had faithfully served her community in the same village corner shop for 50 years. She was beaten to death one Saturday lunchtime in her own store just for a few pounds in the cash register. Another case involved a septuagenarian spinster, who, while fast asleep in her own bed, was raped and murdered.

From 1967 to 1972 I traveled over the length and breadth of the county of Lancashire investigating many sordid murders, and I became very cynical and bitter about human nature and life in general. In early January, 1972, our Task Force was sent to the village of Kirkham to investigate the murder of a 17-year-old Sunday school teacher named Elizabeth Foster. She had last been seen alive shortly before 6:00 p.m. the previous Sunday, standing by a local bus stop where she had been waiting to catch a ride into the nearby town of Preston. She had intended to go to evening worship at a Preston church with a girl friend who lived in that area. The young girl never arrived in Preston, and initial inquiries quickly established that she had not in fact boarded the bus. Later her body was discovered behind a hedge in the picturesque hamlet of Wrea Green, just a mile or so from the bus stop where she had last been seen.

Medical and scientific examination of her body revealed that she had been raped and murdered. Seminal stains were found on her person, and from these the science laboratory determined that her assailant was of an extremely rare blood group. Only one person in ten had this particular blood grouping.

In carrying out the investigation, the police decided that a saliva sample must be obtained from every male person interviewed. From the sample the blood group could be determined. By this method nine out of ten people could automatically be eliminated, and this was the most vital clue we had.

All told, counting both uniformed police and plainclothes detectives, approximately 200 men were involved in the manhunt. An organized system and proven pattern of investigation was rapidly set in motion. Men were assigned to various squads with specific areas of responsibility. These squads, each under the control of a chief inspector, included house-to-house units whose job it was to trace and interview all members of every household in the village and ascertain their movements from the time the victim had last been seen alive until the time her body was discovered, which was many hours later. This was painstaking work in winter weather and demanded much self-discipline, diligence and patience. But over the years this procedure proved to be one of the best methods of detecting vital information. There was also a follow-up inquiry squad, which pursued any useful lead obtained from the house-to-house squads. In addition were the reinterview squad, the *modus operandi* suspects squad, the search team and scene control squad, the specialist squads, and the background inquiry squad. I was assigned to the background squad.

Facing the bus stop where Elizabeth had disappeared were a number of houses. Most of the occupants had been home that early Sunday evening, but none of them had heard any shouts, screams, or other indications of a struggle. There had been no squealing of car tires or other unusual sounds, and the possibility of a forcible abduction appeared rather remote. We had been told that due to her Christian upbringing and training she definitely would not have accepted a lift from a stranger.

Therefore one of the lines of inquiry we vigorously pursued was to trace the male persons with whom the girl was acquainted, as she could have voluntarily and unsuspectingly accepted a lift from someone she knew and trusted. The background squad to which I had been assigned was given the job of tracing every male person that had ever at any time come in contact with her.

From the outset, the girl's character had been painted pure white by those who had known her. Some of us were rather dubious concerning this "paragon of virtue" picture which had been painted of Elizabeth. But as the weeks went by, our doubts were permanently dispelled and the dead girl's past life and conduct shone out radiantly like a beacon on a dark night. Admiration and deep-lasting impressions were created in the minds of many of the hard-bitten detectives on the case because of the girl's purity of life and personal piety.

We were helped enormously by the fact she did not visit dance halls, cinemas or public houses, and she had no boyfriends. Apart from her own family and few personal girlfriends, most of her time had revolved around church activities. Consequently, for the next eight weeks much of my time was given to visiting various churches she had contact with. I interviewed literally dozens of men of all ages.

The procedure for every person had a set pattern to it. After obtaining a written statement from each person. A saliva sample was secured. This process required the individual to pass saliva from the mouth into a small cylindrical-shaped glass bottle which then had to be boiled in water for 10 minutes. This had to be done within 10 minutes of taking the sample so that blood groupings could be correctly determined when later analyzed at the laboratory. Since we did not have time to take each individual sample back to the police station for the boiling process, we carried out the procedure in the interviewed person's own home by putting a pan of water on the stove and placing the glass bottle, suitably labeled with the person's name and address, in the boiling water for the required ten-minute period.

During this waiting time we inevitably had a cup of tea. I found many of the people very friendly, and we passed the time of day discussing many topics — the weather, where we were planning to go for our holidays, what type of motor car we were running and whether we were satisfied with it, who our favorite soccer star and team were, and so on. I suppose that over those weeks almost every subject imaginable was covered — but not one of these churchgoers ever said a word about the Bible or Jesus Christ.

During the ninth week of the investigation, on the evening of the ninth of March, I went to the home of the man who was in charge of the Jehovah Witnesses in the Kirkham area. We had received a rather belated report that Jehovah's Witnesses had been seen in the area on the Sunday evening the girl had disappeared, and my job was to find out who those people were and to interview them in the same manner as everyone else.

This particular man, known as an overseer, lived a few miles away in a village called Freckleton. I remember being impressed with the unusual bungalow as I walked up to the front door. It was all made of wood! I later learned it was Norwegian pine, and that the house had been won in a competition in which the object had been to describe the ideal wife. He and his wife told me they had won it by using the words contained in the Holy Bible in the book of Proverbs, which described the ideal wife!

When we had completed the official side of my visit and were having our customary cup of tea, we engaged in conversation. But this man was not concerned with discussing the niceties of the British weather or the prospects of a continental holiday or the make of his current motor car. Instead, he immediately turned to the Bible and began to talk to me about it and quote passages from it. It had been 13 years or so since I had last seen the Bible opened. I was probably somewhat cynical about it, even if I did not reveal this to the man. I recall asking many questions, drawing on my considerable experience of life as a police officer, and I fired some "hot chestnuts" at him. But, whatever question I asked, he turned over the pages of the Bible with apparently unerring accuracy and supplied me with answers.

He asked me some questions, too. Had I been on the murder investigation since its commencement? I said I had. He asked if I had been in the homes of the people who frequented Christian churches. Again I replied. "Yes." He then asked me if anyone from these Christian churches had opened the Bible, the Word of God, to me. "No," I said. He asked me if anyone from a Christian church had ever visited my home and discussed spiritual matters with me. Again I had to reply, "No."

"No, they won't," he said. "The Christian church has abrogated its responsibility." He said that "Christendom" (as the Watch Tower Bible and Tract Society rather contemptuously calls Christianity) had become worldly and had turned away from the commandments of God and now pursued the way of the world, having spurned godly living for crass materialism and selfish pleasures. He spoke very quietly and didn't give the appearance of being fanatical or having anything of a personal grudge against the Christian church, but was merely stating quietly, soberly, the facts of the present situation. He told me that if I wanted to be sure of being in the right relationship to God, my only certain way was to attend a Kingdom Hall and study with the Jehovah's Witnesses.

I left his home that night quite firmly convinced that much of what he said had been correct. Several things rang true in my own experience. I had just completed eight consecutive weeks of constantly going in and out among men who attended various churches, and it was perfectly true that not one of them had opened the Bible to me or spoken about spiritual matters. I recalled my attendance at my own church as a youth. I remembered various incidents over the years that had left a sour impression upon me, such as the payment of pew rents and the hypocritical conduct which was openly practiced by some.

Now, however, I had been given real food for thought. I had been challenged directly from the Word of God. I was determined to pursue this matter further at the first available opportunity. Could it really be that the Jehovah's Witnesses had the true answers to life and the hereafter? Excitement ran through my veins, and my pulse raced as I considered the implications of it all. Something that mankind had been searching after for thousands of years now appeared to be within my grasp — the way to eternal life!

One morning shortly after this I was in the murder control headquarters when my squad leader called me over and told me I was being taken off the murder investigation. I was assigned to a coordinating committee regarding a forthcoming pop festival to be held in our area in several weeks time. I was astounded and protested vigorously, but he told me that the request had come from the top, and that the boss had consented because of its importance to the Lancashire Constabulary. We had never had a pop festival on our patch before and apparently some people were rather apprehensive about it. It was rumored that 100,000 young people were expected to turn up if the weather was good.

Because of my experience in murder control, I was to collate all the information gleaned at the Isle of Wight pop festival, when approximately a quarter of a million youths had converged on the island. The Hampshire Constabulary had been wise and prudent enough to record everything which had taken place and document it chronologically and comprehensively. My job was to tabulate the relevant facts and then together with the committee, draw up a workable scheme for our own situation.

The task had its compensations — I was given a 9:00 a.m. to 5:00 p.m. office job, in order to do it. I could hardly believe my good fortune. For the past 10 years I had worked a 14 hour day, from 9:00 a.m. until 11:00 p.m., with just one tea time (6:00 p.m.) finish each week. Now the Lancashire Constabulary only wanted my body eight hours a day. They had given me a job in which every evening was free and weekends as well!

For the length of the time I was on this job I took the opportunity to study with the Jehovah's Witnesses. I visited the local Kingdom Hall nearest my home. I remember my first visit. The overseer immediately made himself known to me and told me that his "brother" at Freckleton had informed him of my intended visit. He was warm and friendly in his approach to me and appeared to be genuinely pleased that I had come. The whole congregation made my wife and me feel very welcome.

I attended this Kingdom Hall very regularly during this period, on some occasions three times a week. I studied every training program and service offered, ranging from the simplest for the newest recruits to their most thorough. The main program of study for the body of the congregation was on Sunday afternoons. Here the *Watch Tower* magazine played a very important part. Every week different articles appeared in it, covering many and varied topics. The article would usually begin by outlining the topic and quoting various facts and figures and supplying what appeared to be relevant information. At the end of the paragraph there was invariably a scriptural reference, quoted to substantiate the information supplied. Members in turn would read aloud each paragraph, and then the overseer would ask the questions which were set at the foot of the page. We were invited to answer by raising our hands. I soon found that the answer had to be taken from the actual information contained on that particular page of the magazine — no other answer would be accepted.

My wife was rather unhappy about the whole situation, and I did wonder about the training system, but I quickly brushed all doubts aside. I realized over the weeks that much of what I was reading in both the *Watch Tower* and *Awake* magazines was true. The Watch Tower Bible and Tract Society makes many attacks on 'Christendom,' but I realized that the attacks were justified from purely factual points of view. I cannot recall many of the actual statistics that were quoted, but I know that what the magazine said about falling attendances, apostasy, worldliness and sham was exactly in line with my own personal experience. This heightened my conviction that these people were right.

I also observed their private lives. Were they hypocrites like so many reputed Christians, or had they a genuine belief in what they spoke about, and did they conduct their lives according to their beliefs? I didn't have to be a Sherlock Holmes to discover the answer to those questions! Many of them were totally committed and absolutely dedicated to the cause of Jehovah, to the utter exclusion of anything else!

The case of the local overseer was a typical example. He was the man who conducted a home "Bible study" for several weeks with us. He had been a fireman in one of the midland counties in England. He was progressing quite well as a fireman when an appeal for missionaries was made to his local congregation. There were not many Kingdom Halls in the North of England, and men were needed to expand the work of the Kingdom to vindicate Jehovah's name. This man promptly transferred from the fire service in the Midlands to the brigade at Wigan, losing some seniority and lessening his chances of promotion. But the man did not care. He was only concerned with the things that concerned Jehovah his God. In fact, the move did not work out for him so far as his job was concerned. He told me that the local fire chief did not like "Witnesses" and had made things rather awkward for him, so he had to leave the fire service.

"After all," he told me, "that is exactly what the Bible tells us what will happen to us for the sake of the Kingdom of God — persecution from the world."

He was prepared to take virtually any job he could get, no matter what! The only condition he laid down was that it must not interfere with his evenings or weekends, because those belonged to Jehovah, and nothing must prevent his work for God. He had given up all his personal ambitions; so long as the job gave him sufficient income to provide a roof over his head and food and clothing for his family, he was satisfied. In fact, for his first twelve months or so in the Orrell and Pemberton areas, he, his wife and four growing children lived in a caravan (trailer) not much more than 16 feet in length. He considered it a great privilege to do so in the name of his God.

The whole theme of persecution was given strong emphasis at the Kingdom Hall. The people were told to expect it and were taught how to combat it, or at least to receive it with joy! In fact, there was great rejoicing and a feeling of immense satisfaction every time someone lost his temper with them or slammed a door in their face while they were visiting from house to house. They knew the Scriptures which spoke of persecution by the world. The feeling of being persecuted by a pagan, hostile world which threw its might against just a handful of faithful, pacifist witnesses brought about a bond of unity which I had never seen paralleled in religious circles. The overseer told me that Mr. Heath, the former British Prime Minister, did not like the Witnesses. He was sure the day was coming very shortly when I, as a policeman would be instructed to lock him up because he was a Jehovah's Witness.

His eyes burned bright as he visualized the scene in his mind's eye, and I could sense the ardent fervor within him. He was totally committed to his cause all right!

We had our so-called "Bible study" in our own home once a week. It was really not a study of the Bible at all, but a study of a book called *The Truth That Leads To Eternal Life*. This book propounds Watch Tower doctrines and seeks to prove them by proof texts from the Bible at the end of each theological point.

By the time the pop festival was over, so too was the murder investigation. After many weeks of painstaking inquiries, a bus driver was arrested and charged with Elizabeth Foster's murder. The man had apparently been on the route which Elizabeth traveled from Kirkham to Preston on a number of occasions over a period of several months. During these times he had frequently spoken to her in a friendly manner. On the day she disappeared, he had failed to report for duty at the bus depot as he should have done. Instead he waited until he knew she would be standing at the bus stop and, making sure he was in front of the expected bus, he pulled up in his own car and offered her a lift into Preston. She trustingly accepted, but she never got out of the vehicle alive.

The Living Christ
Chapter Nine

June of 1972, with three months of the Watch Tower's doctrine under my belt and my enthusiasm still strong, I had a telephone conversation with my mother concerning my newfound beliefs.

I had never been a "mummy's darling" or ever fastened to her apron strings, but I did respect both her and my father. When I told her the direction in which my life was now moving, she immediately expressed concern for me. She was not a regular church attender or person who openly expressed her religious beliefs, nor did she know very much about the Jehovah's Witnesses — other than the fact that it was extremely difficult to get them off the doorstep once they had arrived. But Mother said to me, "Ken, before you go any further, will you speak to Brian Smith? I don't know what his religion is, but I know that he believes every word of the Bible and goes around telling other people about it."

Brian Smith was an old school friend. He had been one year ahead of me at the local grammar school. It was over 17 years since I had left school, but I still remembered him well enough. I consented to see him, for two reasons — to respect my mother's wishes and because I considered it an ideal opportunity to convert Brian to becoming a Jehovah's Witness! I wrote to him, and we later arranged by telephone for him to visit me at my home on the evening of the 13th of June, 1972. He asked if he could bring a friend with him named Stewart Baugh. I had never heard of the young man but I readily consented when Brian said his parents had been "Witnesses" for many years and that Stewart understood a lot more about the teachings of the Watch Tower Bible and Tract Society than he did and would be better qualified to discuss the issues involved with me.

The two men arrived at our home shortly after 7:30 p.m. on the night of the 13th of June. Our discussion centered around the deity of Jesus Christ. I sought to show that Christ could not possibly be God. I had a number of Scripture references memorized, which in my opinion, conclusively proved that Jesus was not God but was a being created by Jehovah. I expounded on various texts, seeking to prove the Watch Tower's allegations concerning the supposedly erroneous view held by the Christian church concerning the triune God. Why, one of the Society's tracts even openly challenged any Christian to prove his Trinitarian belief from the pages of the Bible!

Brian and Stewart were very patient. They did not seek to win arguments with me. They just sat tight for some considerable time as the hours passed by, until I slowly but surely ran out of steam. Then they started to talk simply about Jesus Christ. Their manner was totally different from mine. I don't recall their exact words, but the general theme was as follows:

God is a God of love. He created man, giving him free will to choose between good and evil. Man rebelled and went his own way. God still loved man in spite of his willful disobedience and sent Jesus into the world to die for the sins of mankind. They went on to say that Jesus died not only for the sins of the world as a whole, but for the sins of the individual person, for their sins and for mine. Stewart told me that everyone was a sinner in the sight of God and came under His judgment. The penalty for sin was death, but Jesus substituted for us and Himself suffered punishment in our place. He paid our penalty in His body and died that we might live. They told me He was the only sinless person ever to live on this earth and that God had accepted His sacrifice.

We then moved into what was, for me, a very strange discussion. These two men told me that not only did Jesus rise from the dead on the third day and ascend into heaven, but that He was alive on this earth here and now and they both had a personal relationship with Him. This was something entirely new to me. No one from the Kingdom Hall had ever told me this! You see, we had studied the Bible only from an intellectual point of view. We had made a study of religion, just like a schoolboy might learn about mathematics or English or history, or a student might study medicine or psychology or philosophy or any of a hundred other topics. I had plenty of information and head knowledge about the Bible and God, but I certainly had no personal relationship with Him! Everything I knew was from the neck upwards. Yet here were two men telling me that they had a personal relationship with a risen, living Christ and that the Holy Spirit of God dwelt in them! They were both very sincere in their belief and conviction. Although I knew nothing of Stewart's background, I knew quite a bit about Brian's. He had been a sensible, levelheaded boy at school and had worked as a bank clerk. For several years past he had been a news reporter and he was now reporter in charge of a local newspaper. I also knew his wife. She, too, apparently was now professing to have a personal relationship with Jesus Christ. Could what they were saying be true? A personal relationship with Jesus Christ Himself?

"How?" I asked, to which they were too willing to explain.

God says everyone is a sinner, including you and me. (Now the Kingdom Hall spoke much about sin, but sin committed by the world at large, not about the sins of the individual people attending the Kingdom Hall.) You have to confess that you are a sinner. That was the first step. Then you have to repent — not only be sorry for the wrong you have done, but genuinely want to turn completely around from the way of life you are leading and go in the opposite direction. You must acknowledge that Christ has died at Calvary for your sins and by a simple act of faith ask Christ to come into our heart and forgive your sins and give you the assurance of eternal life. They said that if anyone prayed a prayer with those four points in it and really meant it deep down, then God's promise was that he would not turn anyone away.

It was 1:30 a.m. when they left our home. It had been a long night. Joan had sat up with us throughout, and we retired to bed together.

Joan soon went fast asleep, but I could not sleep. I was determined to know if what these men had said was true. I got out of bed and knelt down. Here I was, a hard-bitten "jack"— cynical, proud, not given to undue emotion, kneeling humbly like small child saying my prayers. I had not done this for years, not since junior school when I used to kneel every night in my own small bedroom above our hardware shop and recite the Lord's Prayer. I distinctly remember always finishing up with the words, "thine is the kingdom, the parlor (instead of 'power') and the glory, for ever and ever, Amen." I couldn't understand how parlor came into it, but I had faithfully recited it nightly for years.

Now here I was years later, a grown man, on my knees. I do not remember what I said at first. I seemed to be wrestling over something. I don't know how long I remained on my knees. I only remember in detail the last stage when I prayed the prayer Brian and Stewart had told me about. I confessed I was a sinner. I knew it was true even though I was an upholder of law and order! I had led a very selfish life and had given very little consideration to anyone else. The Holy Spirit convicted me that night of my sin. I didn't like the way my life was going. I knew I was not right with God. I did want a change in my life. I did not know how it could come about, but I told God I did desire that change. I told Him I believed that Jesus had died at Calvary on a tree for my sins, and by faith asked Christ to come into my heart and forgive me and to give me the assurance of eternal life.

And He did! There was no flashing light, like Paul on the Damascus road, no heavenly visions or speaking in tongues or ecstatic experiences, but a deep inward assurance that God had heard and answered my prayer through Christ. I knew that the Holy Spirit now dwelt within me and that God had heard. His promise through His Son, Jesus Christ, just as Brian and Stewart had told me He would if I really prayed and meant it. The mystery of all ages, even before the beginning of time, had now been revealed to me by the grace, mercy and steadfast love of Almighty God Himself. He whose very existence had challenged now answered my prayers. Praise His wonderful name!

The name of Christ I had known for years only as a swear word. Every time I used it was to blaspheme. Ironic isn't it — the very person who loves us the most, the person who loves us so much that He even died for us — yet my way of saying thank you to Him was to use His name as a curse and swear word! But He had not held even this against me. He had forgiven me all my sins, and I now loved Him because He first loved me. I, too, now knew Him as my personal Savior, and what a transformation the power of the Holy Spirit was to make in my life!

By the time half past seven in the morning arrived, our normal rising time, I could wait no longer. I rang Brian at his home to tell him the good news. Joyce, his wife, answered the telephone. Brian was still in bed — it must have been well after 2:00 a.m. when he got to bed. But he quickly came to the phone at Joyce's call. I told him immediately that I knew Christ as my personal Savior. He at once replied, "Hallelujah! Praise the Lord!"

I asked him what I was to do now? I knew I was different. Where did I go to from here? Brian told me that I needed to attend an Evangelical church, someplace where the Word of God was preached. He said that he could not stipulate arbitrarily which church I should go to, but he told me there was a pastor named Ronald Taylor who preached and taught the Word of God and who ministered at a Free Methodist Church at Winstanley. I had never heard of the church but I knew that Winstanley was only about four miles away, so I determined to go there. But first I had other matters to attend to.

Confrontation with False Witnesses

Chapter Ten

On the evening of June 14th, 1972, the very day of my commitment to the Lord Jesus Christ, I drove around, unannounced and unexpected, to the home of the Jehovah's Witness overseer who had been my instructor for many weeks past. I drove down the road towards his house, and as I drew alongside it, my heart momentarily sank to my boots. There, standing in the front garden of his home were the overseer and three other people, all from the Kingdom Hall. It was as though the enemy had lined up all his forces against me! Here I was, only 12 hours old as a born again Christian, having to face a group of people whose combined experience must total between 30 and 40 years! I began to question my very reason for being there. Surely what I was about to do was not really necessary! Why not just send him a letter instead?

I thought of turning the car around and driving away as fast as I could, but then in my mind's eye saw my Lord hanging on the tree and dying for me. Until recent years, capital punishment was retained in England for certain types of murder. When sentenced to death, the felons were hung from the neck by a rope until dead. Other countries execute criminals by electric chair, gas chamber, or firing squad. Without exception, all these judicial executions are swift and painless, but the Roman method of dealing with the common criminal was to hang him from a tree. It is one of most painful deaths known to mankind and can take many hours. Yet Jesus, a totally innocent person, had suffered crucifixion for me! I knew then I could not deny my Savior or back out of the testimony I had intended to give. I parked my car, got out, and walked over to them.

"I want to speak to you," I said to the overseer.

He knew instantly there was something different about me. He didn't know exactly what it was but it certainly affected his behavior. In the past, he had always taken me directly into his home, but this time he took me by the side path around the back of his house and into the greenhouse, where we stood among his hot house plants while I sought to glorify the risen Christ. I asked him how long had he been a Jehovah's Witness, to which he replied. "Fifteen years."

I said to him, "Have you got the assurance that your sins are forgiven you? Do you know Christ as your personal Savior? Have you got eternal life as a present possession right here and now?"

He did not look me in the eye, but he looked down at his boots and said, "No man can say that."

I emphatically replied, "Praise God. I can! Not because of anything I have done, but because God offers salvation as a free gift. The Bible says: 'For it is by grace you have been saved through faith — and this is not from yourselves, it is the gift of God — not by works, so that no one can boast'" (Ephesians 2:8, 9, NIV). I went on and asked if he had been a witness for fifteen years and with all his dedication and knowledge still had not got the assurance of salvation, what chance was there for me? I told him I preferred to accept the Word of God which said that I could receive it as a free gift, and that I had in fact accepted it in faith and had my assurance from the Holy Spirit that now dwelt in me, and that my prayer had been answered.

The overseer finally took me into his home where he opened the Bible and sought to show that I had gone back to being a slave of men. But I pointed out it was he that was a slave to men — namely the men and organization of the Watch Tower Society. He turned to Scriptures I never I knew existed in a desperate attempt to turn me from my new belief, but God gave me answers that night I had never dreamed of. I didn't quote chapter and verse but the Holy Spirit gave the theme of the text, and when I repeated it I got him to turn to the Scripture and read it. He was absolutely amazed. It was only 48 hours since our last "Bible study" together. He was the man who had been teaching me and he knew every Scripture I was aware of, because he had been instrumental in instructing me. But here I was making references to many Scriptures he had never touched on. Finally he said. "No man can have taught you all that you know in 48 hours!"

"No." I replied. "No man can, but the living God can."

Sadly, he said I was the devil come as an angel of light, and he utterly rejected my testimony.

I had a second meeting with the overseer in his home a few days later. Again we poured over the Scriptures. But he would not let me talk for long without interrupting. Every time I believed I was making a really valid point, he would shoot off at a tangent to something totally different. Our theological debate did not get very far at all. His mind had been so indoctrinated in the way of the Watch Tower Society that it was completely closed to any other avenue of thought, and I felt like crying out aloud in desperation. How the situation had changed! A few short days ago, he had appeared impregnable and so full of wisdom and knowledge. Now God had devastatingly reduced him in my eyes and revealed him as someone completely and utterly deceived and misled. My heart bled for him as I pondered over all the things he had given up in life, only to be led up a blind alley.

Only one thing of significance emerged from our discussion. This man told me a great many people had fallen away from the Watch Tower Society throughout his time with the

Jehovah's Witnesses, but I was the only one who had ever met him face to face and stated the reason for leaving the Kingdom Hall. He said all the others had either pushed a note through his letter box or just refused to open their doors to him. This was the very first occasion in 15 years that he had been openly told, man to man, the reason for leaving.

I made arrangements to meet the overseer again the following Wednesday night. I told him I intended to bring Stewart along, just as Brian had brought him to me, to really come to grips with their peculiar doctrinal emphases. The overseer at first agreed to the meeting, but when the day came I received a letter from him, canceling the appointment. I still have that letter in my possession. In the last paragraph he wrote:

"One thing we all must ask ourselves, and that is, what is Jehovah's purpose and where do we stand in relation to it? If we only think of our own salvation then we have missed its purpose. Yours faithfully, J. ..."

So, J ... had closed his door to me. I was no longer willing to conform to the teachings of the Watch Tower Society, so I had to be shunned and avoided. Well, if J ... would not see me, there were other people I had made contact with during my time at the Kingdom Hall, and I was determined to visit them and tell them about the risen, living Christ. My defection must have been announced very quickly, however, for I found that no one was prepared to engage with me in spiritual or theological conversations. The people simply but effectively closed their minds and refused to discuss religion in any shape or form.

I then began to see how the Watch Tower system worked. Conform as a zombie and give total, unquestioning obedience to the society's indoctrinations, and everything is fine. But failure to comply totally spelled out rejection. Again I suffered feelings of intense frustration. If they were not prepared to talk with me, what chance was there of declaring the gospel of Christ to them? How could they possibly be converted and saved from their sins?

Then I remembered my old police inspector at Kirkby. I knew his wife was a Jehovah's Witness, and I had heard that the practice of the household was not to celebrate birthdays or give presents to one another at Christmas. He had now retired from the police force but I knew he lived not very far away, quite close to the town of Preston.

I soon located his address and called at his home one afternoon. He received me warmly, and we talked about old times, and the men we had worked with during those years of the early sixties. Some had now been promoted, some had resigned and left the force, others had retired and were now drawing their police pensions like him, and still others had since died.

I then told the retired inspector of my studies at the Kingdom Hall and then of my conversion and commitment to Christ, resulting in my disassociation with the Watch Tower Society. I asked him for permission to call back again and bring Stewart with me so that we might search the Scriptures together. It was then that I came to the realization that this authoritarian police boss was not master in his own house! In reply to my request, he immediately referred me to his wife and said that it was she I must talk to and not him. He gave the impression that he had no connection with the society. In reality he was dominated by his wife's beliefs and paid lip service at least to the Watch Tower organization.

When I spoke to his wife, she readily consented to the meeting, and we set a date. Later when Stewart and I arrived we met not only the retired inspector and his wife but two other men as well. One of them I knew, for he too was a retired policeman from Kirkby.

We spent the night pouring over the Scriptures and seeking to establish the deity of Christ and the absolute necessity of having a personal relationship with Him. Stewart was marvelous. Whatever the theological issue was raised, he was more than a match for all of their combined experience and Watch Tower wisdom. But the discussion never got heated. It was conducted in a gentlemanly fashion, and we parted amicably at the end of the evening.

As I have already stated, the door was firmly closed to us in my own area as far as declaring the gospel to the Jehovah's Witnesses was concerned. I remember one occasion, though, when I had made arrangements for Stewart and me to go and see the wife of one of the Witnesses. She herself did not follow the Watch Tower teachings and attended the local Anglican church. We did not know how she stood in relationship to Christ. Our intention was to declare the gospel to her and to point out the errors of the Watch Tower Society in order to help her talk to her husband. If he would not speak to us directly, then we would endeavor to assist his wife to do so. When we arrived at her home, however, she was not in, and we could not locate her.

Stewart had come over especially for the meeting, and we wondered what to do with the time now at our disposal. I then remembered a good licensee friend of mine who had suffered his fifth stroke. He lay in a hospital bed paralyzed down one side, and he had lost the use of his speech. The hospital was only 'round the corner,' so we went to see him.

He recognized me instantly and smiled. I gripped his good hand and shook it. I introduced Stewart and then made a silent prayer as I sought to declare Christ to him.

F ... was about 60 years of age and had been a Roman Catholic all his life. I gave my testimony and declared the gospel. He listened intently and unwaveringly looked at me all the time I spoke to him. Although he had been struck dumb, his hearing had not been affected. At the end I asked him if he had understood what I had said. He nodded his head and smiled. We prayed with him and then left.

I later visited F ... on other occasions while he was still in the hospital. When I asked him if he had asked Jesus into his heart, he distinctly nodded his head in the affirmative. I wondered. Dare I believe he had been born again and was now a child of God?

F ... did recover somewhat and was able to speak one or two words with difficulty. He was allowed to return to his public house and in one of our meetings I gathered from his faltering conversation that he now regularly took a walk around to the Catholic church where he went in to pray at different times of the day. He had not done this for many years. Did he now have a personal relationship with Christ? Had the Holy Spirit wrought the miracle in his life and given him new birth?

F ... is now dead, and I never got an answer to my question. Eternity alone will reveal it, but I hope and long to see him among the host of saints in heaven.

The last visit Stewart and I made together was to the very first Jehovah's Witness I had encountered on March 9, 1972, at Freckleton, while investigating Elizabeth Foster's tragic death. The Norwegian pinewood bungalow looked delightful as we drove up the driveway. On the surface, the whole setting was one of peace and harmony. Little did we realize we were sitting on top of a very active volcano which was about to blow its top!

K ... was in the act of changing his clothes when his wife admitted us into the house. He came out of the bedroom fastening the cuff of his shirt, and he smiled broadly at us, greeting us warmly. I came to the sickening realization that as yet he was unaware of my renunciation of the Watch Tower Society and of my commitment to Jesus Christ.

His face changed visibly as he listened to me explain the reason of our visit. His eyes narrowed to slits, and if looks could have killed, we would have been stone dead. Then he exploded. Gone was the quiet, sober approach he had used on my first visit. The mask was now removed. The facade was over. We were now seeing the real man. He didn't actually scream at us. He was a cultured man with an extensive range of vocabulary, and he used it to the full as he denigrated our characters — mine in particular.

In spite of the seriousness of the situation, I wanted to laugh. I was used to being called names, albeit not in such vehement a fashion! Stewart told me later that he was fuming inside and wanted to get up and punch him right in the face, but he showed no signs of his inward emotions and appeared very composed throughout.

The final straw came when K ... accused me of being a dog which had returned to its own vomit. I objected to this strongly. I had not returned to anything. True, I had attended church for many years as a youth, but that had been only a religious tradition. It was purely an external form of ceremony and routine which had nothing to do with knowing Christ as Lord and Savior. My belief was totally new. I could not have had a more radical change in my life than the one which had taken place.

The hate showed in his eyes. He was livid. I still longed for him to know Christ as his personal Savior, but such a reality contradicted the doctrine of the Watch Tower Society. K ... wouldn't listen. We left with his abuses ringing in our ears. It was now our turn to be persecuted by the Witnesses, not vice versa as the case usually was.

I have been asked many times how to deal with Jehovah's Witnesses when they call at the door. What Scriptures should be quoted, and how should one answer their false doctrines with correct use of Scripture?

Let me say at the outset that while it is necessary for us to have a thorough working knowledge of our Bible, the dilemma is not purely a question of winning a theological argument. I believe I have 'proved' my case over and over again with them on many occasions, but I have yet to see my first real convert among them. However, that is not to say it is impossible. The Word of God does not return void. Many are being converted to Christ throughout the British Isles. But it does require the miracle of regeneration brought about by the Holy Spirit. We are told that the unspiritual man does not receive the gifts of the Spirit of God, for they are folly to him; he is not able to understand them because they are spiritually discerned (1 Corinthians 2:14). A Jehovah's Witness, like any other 'natural' man, is dead through trespasses and sins. Our motivation must not be to win an argument, but to love. For if he or she does not come to know the Lord Jesus Christ as Lord, Master and personal Savior, then that person will go to a lost eternity just like everyone else who has not committed himself or herself to Christ.

The Witnesses (and many other cults like them who deny the deity of Christ) have a head full of so-called knowledge of the Bible. But it is false knowledge, planted there by the wiles of deceitful men and not under the guidance of the Holy Spirit. Therefore they have no personal relationship with Christ. When one calls at your door, produce your own Bible. When reference is made to a scripture then, look it up and make them stop their conversation while you read the verse out loud. Don't just read the single verse quoted, but the whole of the passage surrounding the verse in order to give the Holy Spirit the opportunity to reveal to you the context in which the words are being spoken. Also this lets the Witness hear the Word of God outside the context of Watch Tower indoctrination. This procedure also breaks up their stereotyped program and disrupts their thought patterns.

Somewhere along the line, prayerfully seek to present the gospel, if you believe the Holy Spirit is leading you to do so. Give a word of personal testimony as to how and when you came to know Christ as your personal Savior. It need only be a short testimony, no more than three minutes long. Practice it. Write it out and repeat it until you can remember it with confidence.

There are several excellent books available which give

detailed accounts of the Watch Tower's beliefs and how to deal with the Jehovah's Witnesses.

Looking back over my time at the Kingdom Hall I have come to the conclusion that there are two main groups of people who are followers of the Watch Tower Bible and Tract Society. There are those who knowingly, willfully, and at times cunningly lead the people into the false doctrine and bondage of slavery to the Watch Tower organization. On the other hand are those people who, originally having a genuine interest in spiritual matters, having sought and not found satisfaction within the Christian church because of apostasy, modernism and liberalistic thinking and teaching, have now been lured into the clutches of the Kingdom Hall. I am convinced that the second group honestly and sincerely believe they are following the appointed course set by God for man.

It could well be that there are more in this second group of people than we care to think about or realize. What a terrible indictment of the Christian church if this is the case! Deceived human beings who are utterly enslaved to the Watch Tower organization present a very grim picture indeed. How fortunate I am that, by the grace of God, I have been rescued from the miry pit. My heartfelt prayer is for them all, by His matchless grace, to come to a saving faith in Christ.

In view of much liberalistic thinking within the church, and with the rise of heresies and cults and the resurgence of witchcraft, the occult and black magic practices, it is extremely important that we as individual Christians be able to present the gospel of Christ in the power of the Holy Spirit and to give testimony to the saving grace of our Lord Jesus Christ. We must be prepared to stand up and be counted, declaring unequivocally for Christ.

Brian Smith, the man of whom my own nonchurchgoing mother, said, "I don't know what religion he is, but I know he believes every word of the Bible and goes round telling other people about it," is not himself a member of a traditional same earnest conviction with which he had served the Crown as a committed police officer. During his detective days he had learned to pull men together in a team, fully appreciating the value and worth of each of them, and motivating them to work together for the common cause. He brought these qualities to the superintendent's desk. It took him very little time to make his vision known and for the implementation of his plans to begin. These included team ministry, lay involvement, church planting goals, support for small churches, early knowledge of appointments and practical connectionalism, to name but a few. He pursued all of these with the zeal and determination of a detective on a case.

Many lighthearted quips have been made about the little black book that he carried with him everywhere he went, and in which he recorded notes of every worthwhile conversation. His "definition" book, so called, was undoubtedly a relic from his crime squad days, but one which, like the owner, had now been sanctified for spiritual purposes and for the Master's use. Ken maintained a vibrant spiritual life, spending an hour each morning with the Lord in prayer and preparation for the day. At night before retiring, he would kneel by his bed and methodically pray over every conversation, activity and happening of the day, including, naturally, those recorded in the little black book.

One of the highlights of Ken's brief superintendency was a three-day pastors' retreat at Littledale Hall, Lancashire, which concluded just four days prior to his final visit to the United States. It was a time of close fellowship with most of the active pastors present. The program included what turned out to be a very spiritually challenging superintendent's address. At one point he reminded those present that they never know when the Lord may suddenly and unexpectedly call them home. In the light of that fact he emphasized that, "we should keep short accounts with both God and man; there should be no outstanding debts in any of our relationships."

church denomination or building. He is one of a small group of people who meet in a weekly house fellowship and who have no denominational affiliations. If God can use such a small, unstructured group with no resident pastor or plentiful supply of income, how much more should those of us who have these facilities at our fingertips be mindful of our privileges and responsibilities in faithfully proclaiming the gospel!

When did you last witness about Christ? Have you firmly nailed your colors to the mast? Do your neighbors and work colleagues know of your commitment to a risen Lord?

I do not suggest that one must always be talking of Christ every moment to everyone. But when did you last pray, "Please Lord, give the opportunity some time today to share Jesus with someone" — and then be alert for God's answer to that prayer. We must be able to recognize the opportunity when He gives it and not let it slip from our grasp.

While all these incidents had been taking place with the Jehovah's Witnesses. I had not been inactive in other fields. In answer to my question about which church I should attend. Brian had suggested I try the Free Methodist Church at Winstanley. I had been a nominal attender of the local Anglican church, although in the three years or so we had lived in the area I do not think we had attended more than five or six times. The vicar had been very friendly to us and had sought to welcome us into the parish community. But I could not recall that he preached the gospel of Christ. However, since I did not want to be hasty in my judgment, I rang him up and made an appointment to see him. I wished to learn his views about personal salvation and the gospel of Christ. Just fancy that, me interviewing the vicar about religion! That was a turn up for the books!

I had been in conversation with him only a few months previously. I had had the audacity to inform him that he required far more from the people than I did, for as vicar he wanted them inside his church; whereas, I as a policeman only wanted them to refrain from breaking the law! Yet here I was, just a few short months later, investigating the vicar himself to find out if he was a real man of God or just pretending to be one.

He could not give me any real assurance of his own salvation, and at the end of some forty minutes or so during which time I had asked him some very pointed questions, I believe he was heartily relieved to show me the door and to see my back disappearing down his driveway.

I had received the answer I sought, and so I decided that I must try the Free Methodist Church at Winstanley, the one recommended to me by Brian. I had never heard of either pastor Ronald Taylor or the denomination, but I knew that God would make it clear to me where my spiritual home should be. So I made this church my next port of call. In fact, it became my permanent base. I knew from the moment I entered into that gathering of God's people that it was to be my regular place of worship.

Six weeks after my conversion, my wife Joan made a commitment to Christ at one of the services. This was not in response to any appeal, but just a decision made quietly in her own heart while sitting in the pew, and how I rejoiced when she told me that the grace of God had found her too through Jesus Christ!

Many incidents were to occur in my life as a detective in the Lancashire Constabulary as I sought to be a Christian believer within the police force. These incidents were to cause me to be on my knees praying earnestly every morning, asking God to uphold His promises as I sought by His grace and power to resist the three most powerful enemies of the Christian — the world, the flesh and the devil.

Skelmersdale
New Town
Chapter Eleven

Shortly after my commitment to Christ. I received a telephone call from my task force commander.

"Ken. How would you like to go back into sectional operation duties?"

This suggestion was totally unexpected. There had been no inkling whatsoever that this was in the wind. But I knew exactly what he meant. He was asking me how I felt about coming off the task force and moving back into sectional work. I would be responsible for every aspect of criminal investigation for a local community, not specialized like the task force in which I had served for the past five years.

I did some quick thinking. Was this his idea? Did he want me to accept? Was he testing my loyalty to his squad? What if I said the wrong thing? I knew I was close to promotion, and I did not want to jeopardize my chances while on the last lap.

And then I thought. "What am I worried about? Tell him the truth!"

"I wouldn't mind, Sir," I replied.

"How about Ashton?"

"Yes," I promptly responded. Ashton was a small town about four or five miles from where I lived, and it was reckoned to be an easy one.

Then the superintendent said to me. "Or Skelmersdale?"

Now Skelmersdale was an entirely different kettle of fish. It was a rapidly growing new town consisting of large, queerly-designed housing estates occupied mainly by Liverpool-born people who had been compulsorily moved there by the city authorities in one of their slum clearance programs. In a vain attempt to provide jobs for these thousands of folks, an industrial complex was being developed. But I knew the town carried a high unemployment rate, especially among its youth, and that crime was on the increase. This indeed would be a test of my calibre. But I knew there were far more opportunities to do good police work at Skelmersdale than at Ashton, so I unhesitatingly replied, "Yes Sir!"

I reckoned that, if I proved myself to be the man for the job, 'Skem' (as it was known locally) was the place to go in order to stand the best chance of promotion to detective inspector. And that was the job I had pursued with vigor ever since I began with the C.I.D. I decided that this was the only life for me from now on.

I took up my new appointment at the end of July, 1972. My pedigree at that time was as follows: 14 years a policeman; 10 years a crime investigator (five of which had been on crime squad and task force); five years a detective sergeant and six weeks a born-again Christian.

The police station was an old converted house. It was a far cry from Knowsley Hall with its spacious accommodations and green lawns. The building was totally inadequate to handle the personnel now using it. Even though we were considerably under strength, our staff totaled well over 40 people. Conditions were extremely cramped, and I knew the premises were not complying with several of the provisions of the Factories Act, and if the local factories inspector came around he would be within his lawful rights to close the place.

There was only one inside toilet, and it was kept locked and reserved for the exclusive use by the female staff of one cleaning lady, two policewomen and the station typist. Outside in the yard were two other toilets and an old fashioned iron urinal which was not fully enclosed. There was no wash basin in the whole of the building, so the men were obliged to use the kitchen sink, whether for washing our hands or for washing our pots and utensils after eating a meal! We had no staff canteen but only two gas stoves on which to cook meats. A refreshment room was provided, but it was not really large enough to cope with the demand during the lunch hour.

The converted house contained a small corridor leading to three cells. Two of these I found contained a curious assortment of all manner of property, ranging from ancient rusty bicycles and battered perambulators to oxyacetylene cutting gear and tins of chopped ham. When I inquired why the cells were being so used I was informed that there was no inside property store room, and since the sub-divisional superintendent had banned the use of the cells for holding prisoners because they did not comply with home office regulations, they were using them as the store room. So I had nowhere to detain a prisoner in the police station! When I asked what I had to do when I wanted to keep a man in custody over night, I was told I would have to take him to the Ashton Police Station — a round trip of 20 miles or so.

I saw history repeating itself all over again. My mind went back to Kirkby in the early sixties. But I was determined that, as far as I was concerned, it would not repeat itself in the criminal investigation department. I noted that both the fire brigade and ambulance personnel in Skelmersdale had new, modern buildings from which to work, and I wondered when our police chiefs would wake up to the needs of these new developing townships.

I had three men in my department. Two were officially stationed there and one, on paper, was on the divisional headquarters staff, but because of pressure of work within the section, he had been temporarily assigned to help out. I quickly realized that this manpower was totally inadequate for the amount of crime being reported to us. We had no criminal court building in Skelmersdale itself, and the judicial administration of the town was divided into two geographical sections. Most of our crime was committed in the area which came under the control of the Wigan County Magistrates' Court. This meant my men had to take a round trip of some twenty miles or so just to give evidence in court! The other part of town came under the jurisdiction of the Ormskirk County Magistrates' Court and the traveling distance, while considerably less, still consumed valuable time from my small staff.

To make matters worse, my department had no typist of its own. The one station typist was considerably overworked, making it physically impossible for her to return our reports as quickly as we desired. Consequently my men had to resort to typing much of the paperwork themselves. None of them had received professional training, and they certainly weren't touch typists. They spent many long hours behind desks typing reports instead of outside detecting crime and locking up criminals.

I considered having these men employed thus to be grossly inefficient, so I promptly raised the question of having a typist appointed to the department. I was told in no uncertain terms that this was absolutely beyond the question until the new police station was built. When I said I intended to pursue the matter further, the officer concerned smiled rather knowingly at me as if to say. "You're wasting your time, sergeant, and you should know better than to try."

I was determined to get an increase in manpower as well as a typist. When I asked for an increase in men, I was again told that this was out of the question until the opening of the new station. It was true that plans had been approved for a new building to be built sometime in the near future, but the foundations had not yet been laid, and I knew that even if the project were started immediately, it could take up to three years to complete. That is a long time to work in cramped conditions in a building totally unsuitable for existing conditions, with a seriously undermanned department. I didn't even have a place to put a prisoner!

I felt a sense of frustration welling up inside of me. I was desperately concerned for the welfare of my men, the efficiency of my department for which I was responsible and the adequate protection of the citizens of Skelmersdale. I knew it was of paramount importance to increase the staff as rapidly as possible. But it was easier said than done. Every time I pleaded for more manpower, everyone made sympathetic noises but that was as far as it went. I was told that my requests were not feasible because there was no place to put the men in the existing building, and I would just have to be patient and wait for the new one.

I knew there was only one answer to the predicament. From now on, all reported crimes would be recorded on paper so that the crime figures themselves would warrant the increase in manpower. In fact I had already decided on this policy when I first knew I was going to Skelmersdale, and even before I was fully aware of the exact conditions there, I had been motivated to do this by my Christian beliefs. I had seriously questioned the ethical nature and consequences of reporting procedures many times before my conversion, but I never had the courage to carry out my convictions. Now I felt I must abide strictly by police force regulations. What the regulations said and how one operated in practice were often two totally different things, and I knew that my actions would very quickly bring me into a direct collision with headquarters. I also realized that my decision could cost me the promotion I had sought for so long. Let me explain.

No Cuffing
Chapter Twelve

"**F**ear of man will prove to be a snare, but who-
ever trusts in the Lord is kept safe" (Proverbs
29:25, NIV).

It is common practice for many police forces in the British
Isles not to officially record all the crimes that are reported to
them by the public. The Lancashire Constabulary is, or was, no
exception.

The practice has been as follows: when a person reports a
crime to an individual policeman or at a police station, the
officer must first consult his detective for approval before he
records it officially on paper. This procedure is totally irregular
and against all force regulations. If the C.I.D. man considers the
crime to be of relatively small significance, he very often tells
the officer not to record it, and the crime is 'cuffed' — that is, no
official record of it is made or submitted for investigation for
statistical purposes. To all intents and purpose, that offence
officially has never even occurred.

Why is this? In the first place, the country as a whole is
very crime-conscious. The maintenance of law and order has
been emphasized by politicians at general election campaigns
(we British are rather proud of the fact that our legal system
and law enforcement are considered the best in the world), and
over the past decade or so assurances have been given by the

respective parties that the rapidly increasing crime rate would be reduced. This view is conveyed from Parliament through the home office to Her Majesty's Inspectors of Constabulary, whose job it is to inquire into the welfare and efficiency of the different police forces throughout the country. Theoretically, the central government can withhold its monetary grant from any police force if an adverse report is received about it from Her Majesty's Inspectors of Constabulary. The central government, seeking to uphold home office policy, lays stress on crime prevention, and great emphasis is placed on the crime statistics of the individual police forces. The chief constable can find himself under considerable pressure to ensure that crime figures are, in fact, reduced. The chief constable therefore, in an attempt to prove his efficiency to both the home office and to his standing joint committee, seeks to obtain a percentage reduction in his crime figures over a given twelve month period. His views and policies are passed along the chain of command, down to the rank and file. In a genuine attempt to ensure that crime is reduced, many and varied means are employed. The problem is that seldom are desired results achieved over a sustained period of time. Therefore illegal methods are used in order to maintain the good reputation and efficiency of the force.

Another reason for 'cuffing' is the reputation of the respective divisions and sections within each police force. The annual statistics assume considerable importance when they are compared with last year's figures and when one section's results are matched against another section's. Such comparisons are used to determine, in part, the efficiency of the respective criminal investigation departments and of the individual detective who operates an area on his own. Not only the percentage reduction in crime but especially the percentage of detections are important at this level.

For example, let us take some hypothetical figures. If 1,000 crimes have been recorded in a particular section over a twelve month period and 500 of them have been solved, then the detection rate is 50 percent. This is considered quite reasonable and should not incur wrath from the powers above. If, however, 1,000 crimes have been recorded and only 100 of them have been solved, then the detection rate is a mere 10 percent. Should that occur, heads would roll all over the place! Consequently when people report offenses that are considered relatively minor, they are 'cuffed' and not shown on official records — particularly if the circumstances indicate there is little likelihood of the offence being depicted. For example, a man calls at the police station and tells you that his car has been broken into while parked outside a public house and his radio has been stolen; or a senior citizen living alone in an old age pensioner's flat has had her electricity prepayment meter broken into and a few pounds in ten penny pieces stolen; or someone's bicycle has been stolen from outside a crowded football stadium; or a housewife's clothes have mysteriously disappeared from off her washing line. The list is endless. By means of 'cuffing' many such offenses are never recorded. The object is to reduce the actual number of crimes reported in order to please the chief constable and to obtain a good percentage detection rate to show what an efficient body of sleuths we are, thereby preserving our own necks from the chopping block!

My policy, however, was to ensure that every crime reported was officially recorded on paper, and thus fed into the force computer. This very quickly meant a vast increase in the crime rate at Skelmersdale New Town! I figured that this was the only possible way to get an increase in staff. I well knew that I would inevitably incur the wrath of the powers that be, and I was powerless on my own to stand against the weight of officialdom. But I knew my motives were pure and right and that God was on my side.

A few days after arriving in Skelmersdale I attended the uniform parades as the beat constables reported for duty. I instructed them in no uncertain terms that whenever a person reported a criminal offence to them, and they were reasonably satisfied that a crime had been committed, they need not seek a detective's approval before recording it on paper. They were to do it automatically as laid down in the general orders to the force. I also instructed my own men concerning the policy I was adopting and told them also not to 'cuff' crime. I knew this could make things extremely awkward for them. So I told them I would assume full responsibility in the matter, and that if they were questioned as to what was happening and why, they were to have no compunction in saying that it was on my specific instructions.

As the days went by, the paperwork mounted. It now took all our time to record the reported crime, let alone detect it! I wondered not only how much of an increase the actual figures would show, but what the percentage detection rate would be. Every morning before the start of the routine of the day I was downstairs early, on my knees before God, imploring His assistance in the name of Christ. I asked that He would uphold our detection rate, despite the enormous increase in crime now being recorded and the high proportion considered virtually undetectable.

I knew that, without God's help, I would soon be back out in uniform, and that would be a terrible indictment for a detective. It would mean he either had not been up to the expected standard of the elite corps, or he had been caught in some misdemeanor for which he had been reprimanded by being put back into uniform. I certainly did not want this to happen to me. But I knew there was a real conflict of loyalties and, in order to honor God, there was only one course I could pursue — even if it meant the end of my career in the Lancashire Constabulary.

The months went by. The crime figures continued to escalate, and finally a response came from my divisional chief inspector. He at least had the common sense to realize that more manpower was needed in a rapidly expanding town with a larger than average criminal propensity among its inhabitants, and in him I found an ally. The increase in the amount of crime gave him the opportunity to apply for an increase in men! In this he was only partially successful, but the man who was only temporarily helping out was given a transfer and permanent posting to the section, and two C.I.D. aides were attached on a temporary basis. This took place in early 1973, some eight months after I prohibited 'cuffing.' The time was drawing near for the year end reports, due March 31, and I knew that questions would be asked from headquarters about the vast increase in the number of recorded crimes. How was our detection rate going to fare under this numerical onslaught? I would have to wait and see.

In the meantime, I was working for improvements in our building. My complaints had caused some considerable commotion among the different departments at divisional headquarters, and I obtained permission for the cells to be used to hold prisoners. We had a real sorting out of the junk in them to make room for those who had been arrested. It is a wonderfully satisfying feeling to a detective, when, after days or perhaps even weeks of painstaking investigation, he solves his case and arrests his man. Unfortunately, unlike the television play or radio program, the story does not end there, and in one respect his work is only starting. He now has to move from the practical aspect of criminal detection to the academic aspect of recording everything on paper in compliance with the complicated and sometimes tenuous rules of evidence. A good all-round detective has to be extremely versatile. Not only has he to be adept at 'feeling collars' (making arrests), but he must also have sufficient administrative acumen to satisfy the demanding judicial system with all its legalities and complexities.

Teetotal
Chapter Thirteen

On the night of the 21st of September, 1972, just over three months after my conversion and commitment to Christ, I retired to the bedroom and, as usual knelt by the side of the bed to commune with God. I was deep in prayer when a 'voice' said to me. "Ken, I want you to give up drinking." I listened and again I heard. "I want you to give up drinking."

Now the 'voice' was not an audible one, but something which came from deep within and impressed itself upon my thought pattern. I said silently, "Lord, if that's You, You know that I cannot stop drinking. I have been a slave to the habit for over ten years now. You are the God who knows everything about me, even my innermost thoughts. You know that I have tried many times to give up the habit over the years but I cannot. I confess that I am a slave to it."

The same thoughts persisted, however, and try as I might I could not get peace about it until I said. "All right, Lord, if that is what you want me to do, then I am prepared to try. But you will have to give me the strength to do it, because I can't on my own."

Once I had consented with my will, peace returned and I slept undisturbed through the night.

The following morning, arriving at the station as usual, I

declared to my colleagues that I had 'gone on the wagon.' This statement was greeted with some humorous smiles! No sarcastic comments, but I guessed what was going through my men's minds. How often they had heard this said in the past, or had even proclaimed it themselves, especially the morning after a night out on the town. This had happened even to the best of us from time to time. But later the old habit quickly reasserted itself. It was like a magnet to which one is irresistibly drawn, and it was seemingly impossible to avoid being sucked back into its inviting lairs.

"Well, Lord." I thought to myself, "I've declared my intention and shown my colors. I'm trusting in You entirely for this."

I mulled over how, in times past, I had tried to break the habit in my own strength, only to fail miserably every time. I had never lasted more than two or three days at the most. Not that I got blind drunk every night, for I did not. But the habit was so ingrained that I just had to go and have a drink sometime during the evening, even when I was at home off duty. My wife must have despaired many times as she saw me get up and don my coat to leave her for the company and bright lights of the public house.

To be quite honest, I never really imagined what life would be like without doing the rounds of the pubs every night. What was I going to do with my time instead? I knew I had more than enough paperwork to keep me busy, but the job was so demanding and, at times, frustrating. The pub was a wonderful safety valve for unwinding from the pressures of the day. In a way, it was compensation for all the inconveniences a C.I.D. man experiences under the umbrella labeled 'the exigencies of the service.' But now I was going to be increasing my 'donkey work' without the welcome release of alcohol and congenial company. How would I survive? I shuddered at the thought, realizing what my statement meant if I was to keep my word before God.

About 8:30 p.m. that first night on the wagon the men said they were going out on their rounds as usual. I told them to make sure they kept in touch with the station so they could be reached in case of an emergency.

They left, and the office was suddenly empty. I went into the small detective sergeant's office and started wading into the mountain of paperwork which constantly seemed to overflow from the 'in' tray, despite persistent assaults on it every day. I had no desire to go and drink, just a strange sensation of loneliness. I plodded on laboriously, proofchecking every crime and file and report.

I looked at my watch — 10:00 p.m. I decided to call it a day and book myself off duty. I went downstairs, signed off in the main duty register, and said goodnight to the station duty constable, telling him I would be at home if anything serious occurred.

I drove home, put the car in the garage, and entered the house. Joan was quite surprised to see me home so early, and she said so. I'm not sure now whether I had told her at that stage what I had promised God about stopping drinking, but I know we shared an enjoyable hour talking together before we retired to bed.

Sunday came. I worked until 5:00 p.m. and then left word at the office that I could be contacted at my church if required. We attended evening service as a family. I returned to the office about 8:30 p.m. and again worked solidly alone in the office until 10:00 p.m., then went home. So the weekend passed. The first 48 hours were over, and I was still holding good with God. I had suffered no withdrawal symptoms or craving for the beer and had really enjoyed the extra leisure time at home with my wife.

The days passed quickly and, by the grace of God, my resolution stood firm. All my men could see I was serious about my declaration, and they soon gave up asking me if I wanted to go for a drink with them. Then it reached the ears of my boss. He came out one Sunday morning, and we had quite a friendly chat together over a cup of coffee in my office. He brought the subject up, and I confirmed that I no longer took a drink. He wanted to know how I could continue to know what was going on in my rapidly expanding section without making the rounds of the pubs.

"It was a personal decision of mine, and I have not tried to impose my views on the men," I said.'They still conform to the system. Besides, there is so much paperwork coming in that to do the job efficiently I have to work late into the evenings anyway!"

He asked me why had I given up drinking, and I said it was because God had asked me to. I believed the reason was that I was a slave to the habit. I went on to say that the Bible teaches that the body is the temple of the Holy Spirit and should not be defiled, whether with habitual drinking, smoking, drugs or even overeating. I gave the credit to the Lord for the amount of time I had already been off the beer, informing my boss that I had never managed more than two or three days previously.

He shrugged his shoulders. "I don't accept that, Ken," he said. "It's your own will power."

"No, Sir," I replied firmly."It is not, and I am not letting anyone go unchallenged who says it is."

He laughed good humoredly and the subject closed.

I really began to appreciate getting home 'early' in the evenings. Sometimes I would finish promptly at 9:00 p.m. if nothing untoward was happening. Instead of making a beeline for the boozers, I would head straight for home.

During these early months of conversion, God dealt radically not only with my drinking habit (to which I never had the slightest desire to return); he also improved my marriage relationship with Joan. Our marriage had always been strong. It had never floundered, for which I must give my wife the credit. She had uncomplainingly put up with my absence during our children's formative years, and she always greeted me with warmth and affection, whatever time I landed home. I loved her and always had. But I loved her in a very selfish way, always taking her for granted. Now I found that as I worked at my marriage, getting involved in family responsibilities and recreation, a new sense of loyalty and devotion grew within me both to Joan and toward our three growing boys.

Incidental Expenses

Chapter Fourteen

Every month it was my responsibility to check all the returns submitted by my men's expense claims for car and meals allowances, traveling costs and incidental expenses. Every detective without exception in the Lancashire Constabulary claimed his incidental expenses. This meant submitting a special green colored book, issued individually to all C.I.D. men, in which details were recorded of money spent in buying drink and cigarettes in the course of cultivating contacts and informants while making the rounds of the public houses. The maximum amount allowed each month was only two pounds, or 50 pence per week — just over four dollars a month!

At the end of September I submitted my claim for the first 21 days when I had been frequenting the bars. The claim was somewhere around the 1.50 pound mark. In October I never set foot inside a public house and so had not spent any money on incidental expenses. At the end of the month I sat and looked at my book. Very deliberately I wrote in it, 'October 1972 - nil return,' and signed it — knowing mine would be the only book of a working detective in Lancashire to register a nil return.

I checked all the mens' expense sheets and submitted them en bloc as usual.

The following day the telephone rang in my office. I picked

it up and answered. It was my boss.

"Ken," he said, "you've sent your incidental book in, and you haven't claimed any money."

"No, Sir. That's quite right. As you know, I no longer drink and have not been going into the pubs, so I have nothing to claim."

"I think you've made a mistake," he said coolly. "I'm sending the book back so you can make it right." Then the phone suddenly went dead.

Sure enough, the book arrived back on my desk the next day. I looked at it thoughtfully. I opened its pages and reread the last entry in it: 'October 1972 - nil return.' Deliberately I shut the book and placed it in my 'out' tray.

The next day the telephone rang and I answered it. It was the boss again. This time his voice was harsh and almost menacing.

"Stop rocking the boat," he said. "You're the only jack in Lancashire that isn't claiming incidentals! There will be awkward questions raised at headquarters. People will say that if one detective can manage without the money, so can the rest. I'm sending the book back out again and you'd better put it right! The superintendent has already been speaking to me about you, and he says if you don't get round the pubs you're not doing your job properly, and you'll have to get out of the department."

So the die was cast. The book arrived back on my desk once more. I considered my position. If I didn't fill it in and make a claim, then I could say goodbye to my chance of promotion, and even my present job was threatened. Why cause all this fuss? After all, was it worth fighting over 50 pence or the equivalent of one dollar a week?

But I knew it was more than 50 pence. It was the principle. If I filled in the book with false information, then I was telling a lie. If as a result of those lies I was given money, then I had obtained it under false pretenses, which would be a criminal offence. In effect, stealing from my employers.

I knew only too well what the Bible said: 'You shall not steal.' Full stop. Period. The amount was immaterial, whether 50 pence, 50 pounds, or five million pounds. I knew this was the first real showdown since I had become a Christian. Was it worth sacrificing my career, something I had strived for with might and main to the exclusion of everything else for over 14 years, all for the sake of 50 miserable pence a week?

But I was determined not to be dishonest. We frequently had to prosecute others for stealing goods from supermarkets and self-service stores and often the amount was considerably less than 50 pence. What kind of policeman would I be, having been placed in a position of trust and authority, to betray that confidence by committing a serious criminal offence? That would make a mockery of justice.

I turned my thoughts to my Savior again, and I saw Jesus' total, utter commitment for me, even to the extent of voluntarily dying a criminal's death in order that I might be rescued from sin and death and be reconciled with God. "The reason my Father loves me is that I lay down my life --only to take it up again. No one takes it from me, but I lay it down of my own accord" (John 10:17, 18a, NIV). Jesus never asks of us anything He, Himself has not already done. I knew that if my faith was going to have any real meaning and depth, then I had only one course of action. No matter what the consequences, I again sent the book back to divisional headquarters with the same entry: 'October 1972 - nil return.'

I waited with baited breath, but no call came from the boss. My usual procedure was to speak to him most mornings regarding the prisoners arrested overnight and details of crimes committed. This I continued to do, but he didn't mention the topic of the incidental expenses. I thought perhaps he was taking a new line of approach and playing the waiting game, making it a war of nerves. I felt as if the sword of Damocles was suspended over my head. I knew that if I tried to fight the system in my own strength, I would lose hands down, and this I acknowledged on my knees every day before Jesus Christ, and I promised that if God upheld me I would give Him the glory.

I never heard anything further concerning the incidental expenses report throughout the two years I remained a police officer. I continue to praise God and give Him all the glory, even as I did then.

Christmas Eve, 1972

Chapter Fifteen

I t was shortly after lunchtime on Christmas Eve, 1972. The telephone rang in my office. It was the boss.

"Ken, I'm coming out to buy you and the lads a Christmas drink. I'll see you at the pub in about half an hour."

"Very good. Sir." I replied. "I'll pass the invitation on."

I did so and told my men to give the boss my apologies for my absence. They left the office at the appointed time, but had not been gone ten minutes when my telephone rang. It was the boss.

"Sergeant," he said.

Look out! I thought. When the boss starts giving you your rank, fireworks can start to fly.

"I thought I gave you an invitation to come and have a drink with me," he said.

"You did, Sir, but as you know I no longer drink, and I would rather not. I have a lot of paperwork to get through and I'm trying to get reasonably straight for tonight."

"Sergeant," he said. "That was an order!" And he hung up.

I left the office, climbed into my car and drove to the pub. I had not taken an alcoholic drink for nearly three months now, and I was determined not to start again at this juncture. But what would be the cost?

When I arrived at the pub the ale was flowing freely and

the air was blue with smoke. It was a typical working man's pub — a drinking room with a long wooden bar. On the bar were several beer pumps from which the barmaid was filling pint and half-pint glasses. In one corner of the room was a dart board, and several men were sitting around a domino table.

My boss and his men had taken over the bar and were lined out on both sides of him. His face lit up when he saw me. "Ken!" he said. "What are you having to drink?"

"Orange juice, please, Sir," I replied firmly.

He stared hard at me and drew heavily on his cigar. "I said, what are you drinking!" The words came out slowly and distinctly.

"Orange juice, please. Sir."

He bristled. "I'm giving you an order. You'll either have beer or, because it's Christmas, a drop of Scotch. But you'll have an alcoholic drink."

"I'm sorry, Sir." I replied. "You can order me into the pub but you can't make me drink alcohol. That is not a lawful command."

When he saw that open force was not going to work, he then resorted to ridicule. In front of my own men he poked fun at my faith, aided admirably by his side kick boozing partner. I won't say what went on in my mind but, by the grace of God, I was able to stand there and take it, drinking my orange juice. Finally time came and I politely excused myself and made for home, leaving the festivities in full swing behind me.

Often I worked on Christmas day, but this particular Christmas I was off duty. I spent the day quietly with my wife and family. The following day, Boxing Day, I was back at work. I was sitting in my office as usual, wading through the apparently endless mountain of paperwork when the door opened and in walked the boss.

"Good morning, Sir." I said, and waited for the bomb to explode.

"Good morning, Ken," he replied. To my surprise he was

very friendly. "You are serious about your faith aren't you," he said presently. It was more of a statement of fact than an actual question.

"Yes, Sir."

"Tell me all about it," he said.

That Boxing Day morning in Skelmersdale Police Station I shared the gospel of Christ with my boss. He listened attentively while I spoke, and at the end asked questions which showed he understood the spiritual implications of the message. He then told me he believed what I had said, but he was not prepared to give up his present way of life and worldly pleasures. He said he would wait until he was near his deathbed and then he would make a commitment to Christ. I suggested that this was a foolhardy attitude to take. If he really understood the gospel, then he was procrastinating and deliberately cheapening the grace of God. The words contained in 2 Corinthians 6:2 (NIV) came to mind and I quoted them to him, "... I tell you, now is the time of God's favor, now is the day of salvation."

From that time the boss never attempted to induce me to take an alcoholic drink. He came out to the town many times to buy my men a drink but he openly acknowledged the sincerity of my beliefs before them and gave me back my respect in front of them.

This was a real answer to prayer and another real reason I had for thanking God. I know it was a direct intervention by God that I was still standing unscathed after these circumstances. Had I relied solely in my own strength and determination to hold out, I would have fallen at the very first hurdle.

Counting the Cost
Chapter Sixteen

We lived in a very comfortable semidetached house situated in a quiet residential area of Orrell. The house was built of best Withnell brick and there was not a breeze block to be found anywhere in its construction. The workmanship was excellent. It had been built in 1965 by a small privately owned company, the directors of which had retired shortly afterwards. There was nothing like it now being made on the market.

Inside, on the ground floor, we had a large lounge, breakfast room, and a spacious sunlit kitchen which was my wife's pride and joy after the tiny ones she had occupied before. The adjoining brick garage was almost thirty feet in length and ten feet wide and could comfortably accommodate two British made cars. Since we had only one car, this left ample spare room. I kept the car at the front end and the back part made a fine utility room and playroom for the children. There were three bedrooms, a bathroom and a half bath upstairs. We had the whole house centrally heated on a fully automatic oil-fired system. With our own gardens front and rear, this was our dream house, and we were very proud of it.

We had worked extremely hard to raise the down payment in order to secure a 25-year mortgage on the property. It had taken us over 10 years of our married life, several different police houses in five separate townships, plus financial assistance from our family, to be able to afford the luxury of our own private home. This was a completely new era in Joan's life, and she thrilled at being free from the shackles of a county-owned police house. Those houses were all similar, even to being painted either blue or maroon. The police image was stamped all over them. Now, however, my wife was known as Mrs. Leech. We were the only police family living on the road and, since I wore plain clothes, we were readily accepted into the community without having the feeling of being branded as 'police.'

We had really settled in at the Free Methodist church at Winstanley, where we had been accepted with warmth and friendship. Whenever possible I attended Sunday services and the midweek Bible study, and participated in the outreach program to the community. I knew I was growing spiritually under the ministry of our pastor, who faithfully spent many hours each week preparing expository sermons and Bible studies, from which I benefited enormously.

As the months passed by, however, I knew that God was calling me into a deeper commitment with Himself. We lived about four miles from the church building, and when I could not attend because of duties it was difficult for Joan and my family. We had many good friends who would help take them to church, but somehow we felt separated from the community to which God had called us.

We considered the possibility of selling our home and moving onto the Winstanley estate itself. Now, from a common sense, materialistic point of view, this was not good thinking! The houses of that estate were nowhere near as well constructed as ours was. The estate itself was isolated from other townships. There were few shops there and many of the houses were said to be situated on top of mine workings! Also, a move would mean the children would have to change schools and I would have further to travel to get to and from work.

I knew, however, that God wanted us as a family to be more deeply involved in Christian activities, and to me selling the house seemed to be the answer. If we moved near the church, we could participate far more freely, and yet I could pursue my career in the police force and still perhaps obtain the inspector's position I wanted.

My wife and I finally decided this was the thing to do. We spent several wearisome days driving around the Winstanley estate, vainly attempting to find a house we liked. There were many up for sale, well over fifty in all, but we didn't seem to be able to find the one we wanted, and we never felt at peace within ourselves. Still we persisted, and eventually settled for a house situated only a few hundred yards from the church building itself.

This house could not compare with our house in any shape or form. The rooms were smaller; there was nowhere for the children to play; the garage could barely take an average-sized car; the garden was only the size of a postage stamp. The houses here had been built on top of one another with a peculiar communal styling at the rear so that it was impossible to obtain any degree of privacy. Nevertheless, we were determined to get involved in the life of this community and the price appeared right. The couple was anxious to move because of the husband's transfer to another district in his employment.

We talked things over and finally made a gentleman's agreement on the deal. We would be allowed six weeks before I was required to sign a contract. This did not give us much time. But I knew that our house was in a highly desirable area where, as soon as houses came on the market, they were snapped up immediately by eager buyers. I had already had a chat with the assistant bank manager who lived around the corner from us, and he had given me his assessment of what the property was worth on current market values. I decided to advertise it privately, and as time was short, I gave it widespread coverage in the area newspapers.

Time passed, but no inquiries came in whatsoever, apart from agents offering to sell the house for us. When the local paper appeared we could not find the advertisement for our home in it anywhere. I had supplied the details well within the time limit required and had paid in advance the full cost of the advertisement. I was rather indignant and promptly rang the paper and voiced my complaint. A few minutes later the newspaper office called me back and told me that the advertisement was in the paper all right, but not among the houses for sale but completely at the other end of the paper, all on its own, right in the middle of a personal loans column!

To make matters worse, contractors had suddenly appeared in the adjoining access road and dug up the whole of the highway to lay a new sewage system, making it totally impossible for vehicles to reach our home. We knew that many people would not ring up directly to inquire about the house but would drive quietly past, and if they liked the look of the place, would follow up with a direct approach. But this completely stopped any such would-be purchasers. I had spent seventy pounds (over 140 dollars) in advertising fees, and there was nothing at all to show for it.

The climax came that same weekend when the couple whose house we had agreed to buy phoned to said they were being pressed to sign a contract over the house they had bought and that my signature was required that following week! I pointed out that our agreement did not require me to sign for six weeks, and I still had over four weeks to go.

But he said that, because of the change in their circumstances, he wanted me to sign within the next few days. In view of the extraordinary happenings of the past week, I felt I could not do this, and so the deal was canceled.

So ended our first attempt at selling the house known as 40 Transide Road, Orrell. I was left licking my wounds, seventy pounds the poorer, with no reserve capital left whatsoever, and back to square one so far as any deeper involvement in Christian community life was concerned.

Our faith had not been shaken, however, in fact I became more firmly convinced than ever before that God had something in store for us. But it was obviously not to go and live on the Winstanley estate. We decided to do some more praying before attempting any more moves.

My attitude toward my job was also changing. I had begun to realize at last that there were other things in life apart from work. And now I found that I was beginning to lose some of my ambition for promotion. Not that I was no longer prepared to accept the challenge and responsibilities of an onerous job. But it no longer seemed quite so essential to become an officer and a gentleman. This was no longer the primary goal of my life.

Year End Returns
Chapter Seventeen

The police financial and administrative year operates from April 1st to the following March 31st. By the 4th of April I had submitted all our crime reports and year-end returns. I had been in the section for only some nine months, and yet the crime figures were up several hundred from the previous year. This meant an enormous percentage increase. No other section in the whole county would be anything like it.

I waited almost breathlessly to see what the detection rate for Skelmersdale was going to prove to be. Last year, prior to my arrival, it had been 40 percent, and this was quite acceptable to the authorities because of the unusual characteristics and special factors peculiar to Skelmersdale itself. But now because of my 'no cuffing' system, and my insistence that every crime be recorded, the reported number of crimes had increased by leaps and bounds. Surely the detection rate would have slumped considerably. How could we possibly maintain even a reasonable average under the circumstances?

I prayed desperately that God would uphold the system. After all, I was only doing what the orders laid down, and surely it was not all that wrong to want to obtain an increase in staff so that the job could be done in a more efficient manner and so that greater protection could be given to the people living in Skelmersdale.

The day arrived when all the figures were published. I scanned anxiously down the list. There it was — Skelmeradale — 40 percent! Praise the Lord! Despite the huge increase in the number of recorded crimes our detection rate had remained exactly the same. So the official system could work after all! I gave grateful thanks to God. My men were dealing with well over twice the number of crimes recommended by the home office as being a satisfactory case load, and yet we had come out unscathed on the detection rate, despite all the adverse conditions working against us.

Noises were now being made to me from certain quarters that I had proved my point and should slow down. I had been allocated the extra man and the two C.I.D. aides. There could not possibly be any more staff forthcoming until the new station was built, so any further militancy on my part was pointless and would be positively harmful to me personally.

I still, however, did not have a typist nor a fingerprint officer. The fingerprint officers were centralized at divisional headquarters and traveled out each day to wherever their services were required. They were on low car mileage allowances, and once they exceeded their monthly allocation they were then paying out of their own pockets in order to ensure the smooth running of the job. So they were rather careful to make sure their presence was really needed before they turned up at the scene of the crime.

Now we had divisional instruction that every burglary scene had to be visited by a fingerprint officer. Every stolen car that was recovered in the section had to be dusted for fingerprints, and the fingerprint officer's visit to the scene of any crime had to be recorded on the official crime report. This presented real problems to me. I knew it was impossible on the present system for the fingerprint officer to come out to every individual burglary scene and recovered car in Skelmersdale. To do this they would need to visit us two or three times every day! And we were at the extreme end of the division. They would be over their monthly mileage allowance by the end of the first week!

Similarly, with my men being so overworked and tied to typewriters because we had no office typist, it was impossible for them to visit all the scenes of crime they were supposed to. The easy way out of course was to simply record a false entry on the report purporting that the scene had been visited by the respective departments, when this was not the case. But this act constituted a blatant lie! I could not condone the practice.

I tried to make my system as efficient as possible, but it was a sheer physical impossibility for all the required crimes to be visited as expected by either the fingerprint officers or members of the C.I.D. I therefore attempted to determine which crimes were more important and to give them priority over lesser ones. When I submitted the crime reports to divisional headquarters, I left the appropriate entries blank. The boss would ring up and complain. I would respectfully tell him that it was physically impossible to visit them all. He told me I would bring down the wrath of headquarters on my head and that I could be accused of not doing my job efficiently. I would point out that anyone was welcome to come and examine the situation and to try and prove it if they could. I was certainly willing to be subjected to inspection, because I knew that everything would indicate an increase in staff was needed.

I submitted a comprehensive report, asking formally for a typist, seeking to prove the necessity of one for the department, linking it with the excessive case loads of my men and the sheer volume of typewritten paperwork which went around my department. The boss said he had recommended my application. But the weeks rolled by and we heard nothing. It appeared the application had been filed and forgotten. The crime figures continued to rise sharply, and although it was still early in the 1973 administrative year, the rate was way up. Distinct rumblings came from people in high places, yet somehow I was still surviving. But for how long?

God's Call
Made Clear
Chapter Eighteen

At the end of August, 1973, I was one of a small party from our church fellowship who attended SPREE '73 (an abbreviation for Spiritual Reemphasis), which was mainly a training program held for Christians at Earl's Court, London. The five-day conference culminated on Saturday with an open-air rally in the famous Wembley soccer stadium with tens of thousands of people present. Over 11,000 people booked to attend the daily seminars, and every evening several thousand more turned up at the Earl's Court for worship, praise and ministries in song. Each night climaxed with a 15 minute address by Dr. Billy Graham.

It was during this week that I realized God was calling me to Bible college. I had to learn more about the Bible itself, God's unchanging Word to mankind. If I wanted to be a committed disciple of Christ, then I needed to know more about Him. I knew I had reached a crisis point in my life after 15 months as a Christian. I knew unequivocally that God was calling. Was I prepared to respond?

We had been told by Dr. Graham to count the cost before making a decision. For me it would mean the end of my career in the police force and goodbye to the inspector's job. It would mean giving up over 4.000 pounds a year and an excellent pension due in only 10 years time, plus the selling of our home.

What did the future hold? One word, humanly speaking, summed it all up — 'Uncertainty.' I had no guarantee of success in my studies at Bible college. It was over 18 years since I had left school, and I had never been academically minded. Several years had passed since I prepared for my last promotion examinations, and I was not accustomed to prolonged periods of study. I had no way of knowing how I would stand up to it all.

Where would we live? I knew that in order to attend college I had to resign from the police force. This meant that I would no longer be in a position to pay the hefty mortgage commitments on the house so it would have to be sold. And how could I find a place for my family to live when I would have no money to buy or maintain a home during the time I would be in college? What happened after the training was completed? How did I know there would be a job for me? Suppose I failed the course and there was no job?

To these many questions I had no answers. I only knew that Christ was speaking to me and calling me to follow Him. After counting the cost, I decided to submit to Him. If He was prepared to willingly die on a cross for me while I was still a sinner totally alienated from Him, then I could do nothing but accept His gracious call and follow Him. Even though all I could see was uncertainty in front of me, my eye of faith told me that He would provide.

But how would Joan take the news? I knew how much she loved the house we now lived in. After moving repeatedly all over the county of Lancashire for more than a decade and having no settled life whatsoever, I knew she now placed great store in having put down roots in Orrell. Here she was an accepted member of the community, and the children were happily settled in at school. It would certainly be a wrench for her.

When I arrived home and shared with Joan my experiences of SPREE '73, she said that as a wife she was prepared to go with me anywhere I went. But she wanted time to pray and think things through.

During that next month, September, we attended the Christian holiday week at Butlins Holiday Camp at Filey, and it was here that God spoke to Joan, and she fully committed herself to the claims of Christ. The following week in our own church service, God answered her prayer with a wonderful sense of assurance as to what would happen to the children in all this. This was a direct answer from God to Joan's heartfelt plea about the children. We knew then that God had spoken to all as a family, and the scene was set for a whole new way of life.

In early November, 1973, I had a successful interview with London Bible College and was accepted for the two-year London University Diploma in Theology. I was to begin in September, 1974. I had 10 months to wait before my college training could begin. I knew I had to stay and hold fast in the police force until that time arrived.

Armed Robbery
Chapter Nineteen

8:50 a.m. on the Thursday morning before Easter, as I walked into the office I was met with news of an armed robbery at a supermarket a few minutes earlier. Three masked men had entered the store, one carrying a sawed off shotgun and another wielding a pickax handle. They had assaulted the manager in order to get his safe keys, but while looking for the safe they had been disturbed by the arrival of another clerk. They panicked and fled empty-handed, but not without seriously assaulting the clerk, as they did so. Apparently they drove off in a waiting car.

We immediately set up road blocks and began house-to-house inquiries in the area. Almost at once we got a vital clue. As the men were running away from the rear of the supermarket, a lady looking out of a window saw one of the men remove his mask. She recognized the man, and supplied so much useful information as to his habits, haunts and associates that in less than two days we found him. He and three others were arrested and charged with the crime.

We brought the men before the local magistrates and had them initially remanded for three days in custody to the police cells. Soon one of the prisoners pleaded for something to read. Time passes slowly in these places with no one to talk to, nothing to read and only four small walls to stare at. I thought the men just might be desperate enough to read even gospel tracts, so I gave all four of them Christian literature. To the one who had requested the reading material I gave a book telling the story of a man imprisoned in Russia purely because of his faith in Christ.

At the end of the three days I looked for any sign of a move of the Holy Spirit in their lives as a result of reading the literature. The same man who had asked for reading material asked me for something else to read, and I supplied him with three other books — *Why I Quit Syndicated Crime, From Prison To Praise* and *God's Smuggler*.

In June, 1974, three of the four men pleaded guilty to the charge and were sentenced to five years imprisonment. The fourth man pleaded not guilty but was unanimously found guilty by the jury. The judge gave him seven years for being the ringleader.

On the first of August, 1974, at his own request, I visited my book-reading friend in Liverpool jail. In his letter to me he hadn't given his reason for requesting the visit. But when I saw him our conversation turned naturally to God. He said he was really thinking about asking Christ to be his personal Savior, but he realized what a difference this was going to make in his life. He said that from reading the books I gave him he knew that a true Christian went about telling other people about his faith in Christ and made no secret of that fact.

"Yes, that's right," I replied. "As followers of the Lord Jesus Christ, God calls upon us to declare our faith in Him through His Son and, when so called upon, we are expected to respond and faithfully declare our allegiance to Him.

The Apostle Paul said, "I am not ashamed of the gospel, because it is the power of God for the salvation of everyone who believes ... " (Romans 1:16, NIV).

Christ Himself said, "'If anyone is ashamed of me and of my words in this adulterous and sinful generation, the Son of Man will be ashamed of him when he comes in his Father's glory with the holy angels'" (Mark 8:38, NIV).

He said his companions in the cellblock would ridicule him. Besides, how would his wife, a Roman Catholic, take the news? I agreed with him that it would not be easy, but Christ doesn't promise an easy life. "In the same way, any of you who does not give up everything he has cannot be my disciple" (Luke 14:33, NIV).

His greatest stumbling block, however, appeared to be that he was not good enough to be a Christian. He explained how he had tried to be good while he was in prison, but that he kept failing and thinking or saying the wrong things.

I took out my pocket Bible and read 1 Timothy 1: 15 (NIV) — "Here is a trustworthy saying that deserves full acceptance: Christ Jesus came into the world to save sinners ... " I pointed out to him that it was because we were not good enough ourselves that Christ had to come into the world to save us from our sins. At this, the Word and power of God seemed to strike home deep within him and right there in the prison interview room he prayed and received Christ by faith as his personal Savior.

Over 18 months have elapsed now, and God has kept this new Christian strong in his faith. We write to each other almost weekly, and at the end of every college term I take his wife and children to see him, and we have spiritual conversation together. Within the next few months he could be released on parole, and I know that temptations will he strong for him to return to his old way of life. I can only hope and pray that by God's grace he will continue to put his faith in the risen Christ and lead a godly life.

Moment of Decision
Chapter Twenty

believe a word is in order here about my reference to freemasonry. I had to ask myself some serious questions about the fraternal brotherhood of Masons after my commitment to Christ. Can I pledge myself sincerely to Christ and another fellowship which excludes Him in its religious ritual? Is it possible for me to worship in the name of Jesus on Sunday and bow on Monday in prayer with those who neither repent nor confess Him? How can I be both a Christian and a pagan at the same time?

As Bishop Paul N. Ellis has written:

> Life is filled with questions of loyalty. When a man marries, he commits himself to an exclusive loyalty. When he decides upon a vocation he decides against other interests which may have appealed to him and for which he may have had talents. And the decision to make Christ the Lord of one's life demands the supreme commitment. Christ must be first, last and always. The Christian dare not pledge himself to any relationship which is inconsistent with full discipleship. The world makes its bid and invites us to unite with organizations, lodges, fraternities, or sororities which make membership dependent upon a solemn pledge of loyalty. Often this pledge takes the form of a secret oath, foresworn without knowledge of all that is involved and accompanied with dire threats of punish-

ment if the oath is violated. The Christian should check and double check when such an invitation comes. A committed disciple cannot afford to get into a bind. He must keep himself free to follow the will of the Lord.

Jesus, in the Sermon on the Mount, condemns the taking of oaths (Matthew 5:34). This condemnation applies to the Christian in a special way for the Christian knows that he is never lord of his future. He belongs to God. He must be extremely cautious about giving a pledge which binds his future actions. A wholehearted surrender of oneself to Christ is the only unconditional demand consistent with discipleship. All other unreserved loyalties will be idolatrous.

Jesus Christ is man's one and only hope of salvation. Many lodges have rituals, prayers, an altar and hymns. Members engage in acts of worship. Chaplains conduct funeral services, but it is not Christian worship. The hymns omit the name of Jesus. The lessons selected from the Bible do not refer to Christ. The prayers are not offered in the name of our Lord. A society may be religious without being distinctly Christian. In the lodge the Christian is confronted with a self-righteous morality which has no resemblance to the free grace of the gospel. If we know Christ as Savior and Lord, we know that the way to justification is not by morality and self-righteousness. Repentance and faith open the door to eternal life in Christ. The contrite heart cries.

"Lord, be merciful to me, a sinner!"

And that man, unworthy as he is, is justified."

(Paul N. Ellis,*To Keep Yourself Free,* pamphlet.)

I therefore tendered my letter of resignation to my Masonic Lodge on the Fifth of September, 1972. It was a personal decision. To quote again from *To Keep Yourself Free:*

"What you do of course, must be your decision. To conform to the authority of a Christian brotherhood without personal conviction is unsatisfactory. You cannot be an authentic person and do so. The church will never have your true, undivided loyalty if you act only because of its demands. The decision must be yours. You must examine the facts for yourself, ask God for wisdom and understanding of His will and honestly decide upon the course you will take. You must act upon conviction. But you can't afford to disregard the issue. Your loyalty to Christ must be without rival. You cannot serve God and man."

The last two statements apply equally to anything in one's life which would divide one's loyalty to Christ and distract him or her from the worship and service of God.

By the grace of God my concern now is not for self, but other people — people who do not yet know Jesus Christ as their Lord and personal Savior and are plunging headlong into a lost eternity. The Bible tells us that it is appointed for men to die once, and after that comes judgment (Hebrews 9:27). If a person is separated from Christ, then he has no hope.

I think of my landlady who looked after me like a second mother when I first arrived in Fleetwood as a single man. The last time I saw her she was in the hospital, in a geriatric ward, devoid of nearly all her senses. She had unseeing eyes and could not talk. She was fastened in a large high chair, just like an enormous baby, and I fed her soft fruit sweets as though I were feeding an animal at the zoo. My heart cried out within me. This was the person who had loved and cared for me when I had first left home and whom I had been so grateful to. Yet here she was, reduced to such a pathetic state. I asked myself the question, "Does she know Christ as her personal Savior?"

I think of the Anglican vicar I had asked about the assurance of salvation. My sincere prayer is that he will, by the grace of God, come to a realization and full assurance of God's mercy and forgiveness in Christ.

I think of my old boss who said he would wait until he was dying before seeking forgiveness. May he not keep putting off the great salvation so freely offered but accept it by repentance and faith here and now before it is too late.

I think of all my former police colleagues, particularly

those at Skelmersdale who gave me such loyal service, and I pray they will turn to Christ.

I think also of all my friends, relatives and immediate family. I long to see them all bow the knee, plead for forgiveness, and humbly ask by the grace of God through faith in Christ for the free gift of eternal life. Failure to do so will have irredeemable consequences for them throughout all eternity.

"Seek the Lord while he may be found; call on him while he is near. Let the wicked forsake his way and the evil man his thoughts. Let him turn to the Lord, and he will have mercy on him, and to our God, for he will freely pardon" (Isaiah 55:6-7, NIV).

What is YOUR decision my friend?

True Liberty
Chapter Twenty-one

The year-end returns published in April, 1974, again showed a tremendous increase in the actual number of recorded crimes in Skelmersdale — so much so that an increase in strength was authorized for our criminal investigation department. The staff additions would include one detective inspector, two detective sergeants and six detective constables. Also a typist was finally allocated to us, plus a fingerprint officer. When these vacancies were filled the C.I.D. would begin to look something like a department, a far cry from when I had taken over less than two years previously.

In June of 1974 the Detective Superintendent came to see me. He was well aware of my intentions to leave the service because London Bible College had written to the Chief Constable asking for a reference about me. He took me to one side and told me that the police force did not want to lose me, and he asked me to reconsider and stay on in the job. If I were to reconsider and stay on, the rank of detective inspector would be mine!

He went on to say that while he sincerely respected my views, I must remember I had a wife and family to consider. Many people would be ungrateful and would not appreciate my services, and I would get a salary which would only barely keep me off the bread line. He referred to one minister he knew who actually had to rely on charity from his parishioners. Times would be hard for my family, he said. Why not wait nine more years? Then I could retire on a nice fat pension and carry out my beliefs and convictions without being entirely dependent on outside support.

I could not find fault in his reasoning or logic. I knew perfectly well that what he had said was true. Yes, here it was, the job I had striven for with might and main all those years, now being offered to me.

I looked at the Superintendent. "I'm sorry, Sir," I said. "God's call is for the here and now, and I must obey."

Police regulations require giving one month's notice regarding resignations from the force. I typed mine out a few weeks before the required deadline. I had never dreamed for one moment throughout my whole police career that I would ever be typing out my resignation. To me it had been my whole way of life. Yet here I was, calmly typing it out without any remorse or regret. My burning ambition to get to the top had been completely shattered. I wouldn't have believed it — but I had not reckoned with the power of the living God.

As I signed the brief report giving the barest details, the words of a well-known hymn came to mind —*Though the way seemed straight and narrow, all I claimed was swept away; my ambitions, plans and wishes, at my feet in ashes lay* (I Will Praise Him).

Shortly afterward, the Chief Superintendent walked into my office. "Well, Sergeant," he said. "Have you put it in yet?"

"Yes, Sir," I replied.

"When do you finish?"

"Friday, the 13th of September, Sir."

His eyes widened and he said incredulously, "Friday the 13th! What a day to finish on, Sergeant."

I smiled and said, "I remember the day when I was last mindful to superstition, but not now, Sir. Christ has set me free from all that."

Once again we put our house up for sale. This time it sold

very quickly without any trouble at all, although God tested our faith by making us wait until there were only eight days to go before the contracted day of departure from our home. He very graciously provided us with a modest but comfortable terraced house in a small village near Skelmersdale — our present home. The landlady is a Christian, and she and her family have lovingly rendered their assistance to my family while I have been deep in my studies at London Bible College.

At the time of my commitment to Christ in June, 1972, I was a happily married man with three growing sons. We had a lovely home and most of the material goods any person could wish for. The house was full of nice furniture, including a color television, a deep freeze unit, and all the modern conveniences. I had my third new car and was in the habit of changing vehicles every two or three years. We even owned a small boat.

I had obtained promotion in the police force and was in a position of authority. I was respected by the lawabiding citizens around me. The police force had been good to me, and I had no chip on my shoulder. I just knew that, for all these things, there was something vital missing in my life which nothing could completely compensate for. That vital deficiency in my life was remedied in a unique way by Christ Jesus who is now my Lord and Master. It was He Who was missing!

One is either a slave to sin or a slave to Christ. But Christ not only gives eternal life, indescribably wonderful as that is, He also gives a Christian the Holy Spirit whose indwelling power enables him to be freed from all the bondage and fears of this present world and to live a victorious life here on this earth.

I have mentioned in this book a number of people who were slaves to sin of some form or another. I have met people enslaved by habitual drinking, adultery and immorality, numerology, astrology and horoscopes, wealth, freemasonry, drugs, and selfish ambition. All these are ploys by the enemy to keep a person in the evil grip of fear, deception, and slavery to sin — the wages of which is eternal death. I rejoice that the living God has completely smashed my old habits and way of life and has given me a completely new life. "Therefore if anyone is in Christ, he is a new creation; the old has gone, the new has come!" (2 Corinthians 5:17, NIV). Gone even is the haunting fear of death which dogged my footsteps through all those years in the police force. Christ says, "Do not be afraid. I am the First and the Last. I am the Living One; I was dead, and behold I am alive for ever and ever! And I hold the keys of death and Hades" (Revelation 1: 17, 18, NIV). I know by the Word of God that Christ suffered death and judgment for me, and that I no longer come under the wrath and condemnation of God, but have passed from death to life and have nothing to fear in leaving this world for the next.

Christ indeed has given me true liberty. The justice God gives through the blood of His Son shed on the cross at Calvary is a free and gracious pardon to every confessing and repenting sinner, whether king or beggar. He gives the power to overcome the world.

Burning Desire
Chapter Twenty-two

(Editor's Note: These concluding chapters that bring Ken Leech's story from 1974 forward, were provided by his colleague in ministry, the Reverend Colin Le Noury of Preston, Lancashire.)

By no means a proud man, Ken Leech could describe with relish how he had graduated at the top of his class in police driver-training school. Such a skill was a vital one, of course, since driving in pursuit of the offender is one of the two or three most dangerous things a policeman ever does. Part of training was learning how to pay attention. The trainee would have one instructor beside him and another in the backseat. The latter was called the "spotter," and he would make mysterious predictions from time to time. "Around the next bend," he might say, "you will come upon a crippled lorry [or truck] on the shoulder. The cab door is open and the driver is hanging out signaling for help." Sure enough, once the next bend was passed, the scene was just as the spotter had described it. How was it done? Quite simply, the spotter had given close heed to the long stretch seen from the last ridge. He was training the novice to take in a larger picture of what lay ahead.

So before he ever became a Christian evangelist Ken had been well taught not only to attend to the overlooked detail under one's nose, but also to the big picture. His vision would come to include the cities, with his having a brief tenure in London. It would be international, including significant work in North America. He always had a passion for taking new ground and he was a true frontiersman.

A young American engineer, newly converted and called into full-time ministry, recalled, how Ken had described himself to a fellow airline passenger on a transatlantic flight. Asked what he did, Ken said, "I am an ambassador. Wherever I go I represent Jesus Christ and His Kingdom." The imperative he felt was to see that kingdom of grace, forgiveness and new life extended.

But his future ministry was to be grounded in disciplined training, as the case had been with Ken's police work. His new commitment meant he must head off to London Bible College (LBC). This in turn meant major adjustments for the household. Christian work ordinarily involves sacrifice of some kind. For Ken, the sacrifice was his surrendering a well-paid and prestigious career in crime detection. For Joan and the family, it was remaining in Lancashire while Ken settled in 250 miles away in London. The family's relocation from its lovely home could not have been easy. The new residence, which Ken later described as a "modest but comfortable terrace house," was in reality a damp, unmodernized miner's cottage without the luxury of a bath or an indoor toilet!

But, as Joan admitted, God was working in their lives, and He had changed their attitude toward "things." During these long periods of separation, which often spanned many weeks, Joan learned to stand on her own faith — the faith that had led her months earlier to trust herself and her family to the Lord. The faith that now enabled her to say, along with the Apostle Paul, "I have learned in whatever state I am to be content."

Joan's account of her commitment to God's full purpose for her life is an important part of the Leech story. When Ken had announced to her his surrender to God for whatever was wanted, Joan felt a deep unsettledness of spirit. There were three young sons, a fine home to be kept up — a million familiar things to be cared for. She found herself asking God, "Why do men have such *freedom* to make big decisions like this? What about the boys I am rearing?" The tussle with God came to a climax in a morning worship with their friend Reverend Ron Taylor preaching. Joan said her wrestling with God took her wholly outside the immediate scene. She and God were in a time and place apart, in vivid encounter. She felt God was saying to her, "Give me the boys, and then you will know true freedom." Finally she found grace to say the final yes and was at once back in the present, with her oldest son, Kenneth, pushing past her to go to the front to pray. The peace of God flooded her heart. Two decades later she would report, "I've never taken my sons back from God, and God has been faithful in caring for them." She would also report that her surrender meant that if God had asked her to live on the wrong side of the tracks in London she could have done that. The surrender was genuine and complete.

Early on the way, throughout the period in the miner's cottage, Joan was always conscious of God's care and had the joy of seeing persons commit their lives to Christ. Though hundreds of miles apart, Joan and Ken both were being prepared for their future ministry.

While Ken was busily immersed in his studies at LBC, Charles Kingsley, from his vantage point as Executive Director of Light and Life Men International (LLMI) in the United States, was keeping track of developments. He had been present in the Winstanley Church on the morning in 1974 when the young policeman had announced his call to full-time Christian service. He had made a mental note of the unusual promise already evident in this serious new believer. In February 1975 Ken received an invitation to travel to the United States the coming summer under LLMI auspices to share his faith with men's groups. This proved to be the first step in a fruitful and lifelong association with the international men's organization. Many persons who came to know Ken on his first visit to North America became long-term prayer and financial supporters.

The real challenge came at the end of the 12-month period in America when he faced discerning the Lord's will for the future. As far as LLMI was concerned openings were present for further ministry in North America, but in Ken's heart was a burning desire to plant new churches in the United Kingdom. Only 12 months earlier Conference Superintendent Victor Trinder had warned him, "Go to the United States, and you'll never want to come back to England again." But come back he did and fulfilled his most important life's work.

It was an exciting time in the Great Britain Conference in the mid-to-late '70s, with a shared vision for growth. Nowhere was this more evident than in the Garstang Circuit where three established congregations were joining together to plant a fourth church in Fulwood, Preston. Ken, on his return from the United States, was one of two young pastors appointed to the Garstang Circuit under the supervision of Reverend Barrie Walton.

His main focus of ministry was in the area around the Crown Lane Church. When this congregation of 60 full members decided to send two-thirds of its membership to the new church plant in Fulwood, the Leech family moved with them. Without doubt Ken's devotion to wholehearted evangelism was central to the rapid growth and development of this new congregation.

In 1978 while still working in the Fulwood area, Ken received a letter from a Christian friend in Morecambe, some 30 miles north of Fulwood. In it was information on a young couple who had just moved to the Moss Side area of Leyland some 10 miles south of Fulwood. Andy and Lin Parr (now missionary church planters in Japan) had relocated for the purpose of employment. Andy had just taken a teaching post at

Bishop Rawsthorne, the local Anglican high school. Like the detective following up the slimmest of leads, Ken called on the couple and found them to be keen Christians with an intense desire to reach their new neighbors for Christ. The opportunity that this presented was just too good for Ken to miss. With a band of enthusiastic helpers from Fulwood, a systematic program of visitation was carried out. This led to an evangelistic Bible study in the Parrs' home that attracted many neighbors.

Much of Ken's work in the Lancashire Constabulary had been focused on the "New Towns" of Lancashire. Warrington, Kirby and Skelmersdale immediately spring to mind. The Commission for New Towns (CNT) had been highly active in Lancashire during the '60s and '70s, and they continued to be so in the early '80s. Leyland Moss Side was one of the areas that they had targeted in their Urban Development Program. With the large industrial base in Leyland at the time, many people were moving into the new homes on Moss Side in the pursuit of employment. A fine mix of CNT and private housing sprang up in just a few years, and Moss Side became a developing community (though one without an evangelical church).

The town of Leyland itself was close to existing Free Methodist churches lying almost equidistant between Fulwood and Winstanley. Ken was the person who marked the spiritual and social clues that indicated an area with need for a church plant venture.

The germ of the idea was relayed back to Fulwood, to Ken's senior pastor, Barrie Walton, and to the conference superintendent, Victor Trinder. Everyone was feeling positive and excited about the possibility of new Free Methodist work in Leyland.

Part of CNT's program for development in "new town" areas was the provision of facilities to meet individual needs, including the building of multipurpose community centers. The arrival of Ken at Moss Side ensured that the areas had an evangelical pastor who was also community-minded. Within a matter of months Ken and Joan had put their roots deep into the community and had secured the use of the Moss Side Community Center where they began public worship services on September 1, 1979.

One way in which Ken made contacts on Moss Side was by obtaining regular up-to-date listings from CNT of all people moving into the area. These were carefully noted, and all the addresses were systematically followed up. This was done with the same determination and persistence with which he had conducted his home calls during the Elizabeth Foster investigation years before. Upon visiting homes he would leave information about the community and its facilities, including the Free Methodist Church. He seized every opportunity for presenting the gospel on a one-to-one basis.

Ken's style of pastoral leadership and church planting was fresh, often breaking from traditional patterns and always productive. The seeking of the lost, discipling of converts, establishment of "Growth Groups" and the early delegation of responsibility to lay leadership were intrinsic features of that style fully employed at Leyland.

One of the blessings that Ken enjoyed was the fact that he had the full blessing and confidence of his conference superintendent. This enabled him, when he felt that his work in Leyland was nearing completion, to converse with Victor Trinder about the future.

Together they considered some of the areas that might be suitable for a new church plant venture. High on that list was the Lake District, north of Lancashire. One of eight national parks in Britain, it is an area of extraordinary natural beauty. It includes the Cambrian Mountains with some of the highest peaks in England, along with Britain 'Great Lakes' — Windermere, Coniston, Ulswater and Keswick. The region is dotted with small towns and villages.

Strategically, the Lake District was a good target for the

planting of a church or churches, as it would form a bridge between the existing churches in Lancashire and the newly emerging work in Glasgow, Scotland. Unfortunately, there was no clear leading from the Lord. This particular choice, so attractive to the human eye and heart, was set aside.

Where next? This was the perplexing question. It had long been Victor Trinder's vision for the young movement "to create a new sphere of influence." In response to his "Light and Life Hour" broadcasts relayed via Trans World Radio in Monte Carlo he had received correspondence from far and wide. The large percentage of UK letters seemed to be coming from the southwest of England. His suggestion, therefore, was to explore the West Country, an area that had long been a bastion of Methodism dating back to the days of Wesley himself.

The step Ken and Joan took in late summer 1983 was the most spiritually challenging exercise of their ministry. This new assignment involved no hard contacts, no base, no church, no parsonage, certainly no guarantee of success. Ken had a few addresses from the "Light and Life Hour" in hand and a burning desire to begin church planting again.

Cornwall, the southernmost county in Britain, with a native population who are decidedly Cornish first and British second, and where all but Cornishmen are "foreigners," was 400 miles from the nearest Free Methodist church. The sheer scale of the challenge demanded faith, skill and careful staging.

First priority was to get a roof over their heads. They acquired a vacation home in the market town of Truro on a rental basis. From there they were able to explore the surrounding towns of Redruth, Camborne, St. Austell and even Penzance just a short distance from Land's End. All these places had an evangelical presence, and Ken met with many of the ministers and visited their churches. He assured them that he had not come to set himself up in competition with them.

Truro itself was beginning to look like the place that offered the most potential, but unknown to Ken at the time, other praying people had different thoughts in mind.

The Pascoes were a well-known evangelical family in Cornwall. Through a former Lancashire contact and a Christian Literature Crusade prayer group, the Pascoes were made aware of the Leeches' presence and their desire for church planting. Amy Pascoe felt that Helston was the place where they should be, and had written a letter to that effect. Not wishing to be spiritually presumptuous, she kept from mailing it until she was absolutely certain that it was the right thing to do. This was confirmed to her soon afterward when another Christian, Joan Rudder, who had also heard about the Leeches, approached Amy with the suggestion that they possibly should be in Helston rather than Truro. It has been established by the mouth of two witnesses and a letter was promptly sent.

Helston was a town of approximately 12,000 people just a short distance from the famous Culrose Naval Base. It had no evangelical church as such at that time, just a mission with an evening meeting and a small, aging congregation. The Pascoes introduced Ken to many people, including Stanley Plaistow, who in turn introduced him to the St. John's Mission. Ken found a small group of people there who had been praying for 12 months for someone to come and conduct regular meetings in their mission building.

From May 16, 1984, on, Ken was able to use the mission on Sunday mornings for public worship, rent-free, while the mission group continued its own meetings in the evenings. Within six weeks they saw their first Cornish convert, the first of many to follow in the ensuing years. On November 8, 1985, a Free Methodist church was established with nine founding members. The burning desire, yet again, had kindled an enduring flame.

Ken and Joan were greatly aided for two years by a young couple, Ian and Lois McKinlay, of the Crown Lane Church, who were preparing themselves for the mission field. Their contribution in the early days was invaluable as were visits from

groups and individuals from the Lancashire churches. Once
again personal evangelism, home-based Bible studies, growth
groups, and free distribution of the Christian newspaper
Challenge were part of the successful development of the work.

Perhaps the most significant step came in May 1988 when
the mission trustees felt that their work had ended and handed
the building to the Free Methodist Church for a nominal sum.
This was a mark of the confidence, trust and esteem that Ken
had earned. In the span of 10 years, and in new territory, a Free
Methodist congregation was built up with its own building and
parsonage, destined to be debt free shortly afterward.

More than 150 years before, the famous Cornish Methodist
Bible Christian preacher Billy Bray had managed to extract,
from a miser in Helston, two shillings and sixpence for a
church building project. He was so thrilled that he hailed it as
the only miracle that ever took place in the town of Helston.
Today a thriving Free Methodist congregation exists in the
town. Helston's second miracle perhaps? Ken Leech was a part
of that miracle.

Full Circle
Chapter Twenty-three

"Will all remaining passengers for American Eagle flight 4184 to Chicago please proceed to the departure gate?" The urging of the attendant came well after the original departure time had passed. A busy O'Hare Airport at the Chicago hub had meant delayed takeoff for the feeder airlines.

Among those who had already checked in for the ill-fated flight on the afternoon of October 31, 1994, were Ken Leech and his colleague Alan Ramm. It was a cold and blustery afternoon, with the ATR 72 turbo prop rocking in the wind as it sat on the apron awaiting departure. But none of those who boarded it could have imagined what the tragic end of that flight would be. Sixty miles out of Chicago the plane plunged out of the sky and down into a cornfield.

News of the tragedy in Lowell County, Indiana, flashed from coast to coast. Even the early reports gave no hope of survivors among the 64 passengers and four crew members. For Ken Leech and Alan Ramm, hoping to pick up a connecting transatlantic flight to Manchester, England and home, it was the moment of their true homecoming.

Just two days previously, in a memorial service in Indianapolis, Ken had read from the Scriptures in John 14:1-3 (paraphrased), "Do not let your hearts be troubled. Trust in

God, trust also in me. There are many rooms in my Father's house; otherwise, I would have told you. I am going there to prepare a place for you. And if I go and prepare a place for you, I will come back and take you to be with me. ..."

Ironically, during that same week as the two men sat in a restaurant eating a meal with Superintendent Gilbert Ablard of Arizona, the conversation centered on Enoch and his sudden departure as expressed in the words, "And God took him," at which point Ken turned to his companions and exclaimed, "What a wonderful way to go." Truly the Lord had now taken two more men who, like Enoch, had learned to walk with Him.

Just eight weeks before, Ken had been installed as superintendent of the two United Kingdom (U.K.) Conferences of the Free Methodist Church. Alan was the capable conference administrator and Ken's personal secretary. Together they had been attending the annual Board of Administration meetings at the Free Methodist World Ministries Center in Indianapolis.

During the previous 12 months of Ken's life, the Lord had brought a number of things full circle. One of these was the call to church plant in the great metropolis of London. It seems appropriate that the city in which he had trained for Christian ministry nearly 20 years previously, and where he had his first real taste of evangelism at SPREE '73, became the scene of his last pastoral/church plant appointment.

The fact that the work in Helston had been brought to a healthy state of maturity under Ken and Joan's leadership meant the time was right for a new challenge. The Conference Board of Evangelism had been looking for a new area in which to church plant, and Ken, the former detective, had been designated to investigate the possibilities.

A number of ideas were looked into, but the only one that seemed to offer promise was the City of Leeds in West Yorkshire, on the opposite side of the Pennine Mountains from the nucleus of Lancashire churches. Hopes grew and excitement began as Ken led in-depth investigations in the area, but the hopes were dashed by a fruitless response, indicating that the Lord was not opening that particular door.

Soon afterward Conference Superintendent Barrie Walton called the churches to a day of prayer and fasting for church planting and at the united prayer meeting in the evening at Fulwood, it was revealed that a tiny group of believers with a century-old building in Acton Green, West London, were seeking to affiliate with a larger body. Ken had had the first contacts with the group through a Cornish connection and was given the freedom to develop what appeared to be "Macedonian Call" at a time when all other doors had closed. When the time came to appoint a pastor in November 1993, Ken was the obvious choice.

Another circle was to be unexpectedly completed shortly afterward. It was February 1994 when the U.K. conferences were shocked by the news that Barrie Walton was laying aside his duties as conference superintendent due to ill health. He would not be seeking reelection in the coming May. Ken Leech would be a suitable nominee for the post.

Many questions ran through Ken's mind when offered the nomination, notably, "Was this God's will? What would happen to Acton Green?" After much prayer and consideration with Joan, and discussion with the Acton Green Board, Ken accepted the nomination as the Lord's will and was elected in May 1994.

The Leeches left Acton Green after just 10 months to take residence in the superintendent's parsonage in Fulwood, Preston — the very area where Ken had functioned in his first ministerial appointment. Over a period of 17 years they had moved from Fulwood to Leyland, to Cornwall, to London and now back to Fulwood again. Another circle had been drawn to completion.

Although Ken's time as superintendent was short-lived — just eight weeks — it was significant in many ways. At his installation service he made his vows of dedication with the

It was this writer's privilege, at Ken's request, to lead the closing communion service of the retreat. This concluded with all the pastors linking hands and standing in full circle to sing, "How Good is the God We Adore." Everyone sang lustily, no one anticipating how poignant the words would soon become:

"'Tis Jesus the first and the last
Whose spirit will guide us safe home.
We'll praise Him for all that is past
and trust Him for all that's to come."

One other circle that deserves a mention relates to the Kirkham Free Methodist Church. From early days it had been Ken's desire to see a work established in that town. It was in 1984, under my own leadership, that the Great Eccleston and Crown Lane churches began a church plant program in the Kirkham Social Services Hall. Persons were won to Christ, and the work grew. Over time the fellowship moved to different venues, coming to rest in its present location, the Kirkham Community Center. *Ironically, this is the very building where Ken had set up his incident room during the Elizabeth Foster murder inquiry — the event which led to his own conversion.* Strange and wonderful indeed are the ways of Providence.

The passing of this man of God has spoken to many, not least among them his youngest son, Stephen, who recently re-committed his life to Christ. An entire family united in faith — this blessed fact reminds one of yet one more circle:

"There are loved ones in the glory
whose dear forms we often miss
when you end your earthly story
will you join them in their bliss?"
"Will the circle be unbroken
by and by, by and by,
In that better home awaiting,
in the sky, in the sky?"

Reader, if the intrepid detective and dedicated evangelist Ken Leech were here today, he would seek the answer to just one more question: "Will you, too, accept God's gift of salvation and new life in Jesus Christ?"

The steps below will aid you in finding new life in Christ.

1 — Recognize the fact of sin and its penalty.
For all have sinned and fall short of the glory of God. Romans 3:23, NIV

2 — Accept God's remedy, Christ's death on the cross.
We deserve death because of our guilt. Christ loved us and took the penalty for our sins by shedding His blood. Jesus said, *I am the way and the truth and the life. No one comes to the Father except through me.* John 14:6, NIV

3 — Believe (trust in) God's Son and His act of love.
The Bible says: *For salvation that comes from trusting Christ ... which is what we preach ... is already within easy reach of each of us; in fact, it is as near as our own hearts and mouths, for if you tell others with your own mouth that Jesus Christ is your Lord and believe in your own heart that God raised Him from the dead, you will be saved. For it is by believing in his heart that a man becomes right with God; and with his mouth he tells others of his faith, confirming his salvation.* Romans 10:8-10, TLB

4 — Turn from your sins, repent and find His forgiveness.
If we confess our sins, He is faithful and just and will forgive us our sins and purify us from all unrighteousness. 1 John 1:9, NIV

5 — Receive Christ as your Lord and Savior.
But to all who received Him, He gave the right to become children of God. John 1:12, TLB

A prayer of commitment — Dear Father: I know that I am a sinner and in need of Your forgiveness. I believe that Jesus Christ, Your Son, died for my sins. I now turn from my sins and repent. Please forgive me now. Thank You for doing it. Dear Lord, I know You are standing at the door of my life. I invite You to come and take over my life as my personal Savior. I am willing, by God's grace, to follow and obey Christ as the Lord of my life. Thank you for doing it just as You promised in Your Word. In Jesus name, Amen.

The new life with Christ — If you have sincerely prayed this prayer, God has just given you new life. You have become a child of God through Jesus Christ. A member of God's family. In 2 Corinthians 5:17 it says: *Therefore, if anyone is in Christ, he is a new creation; the old has gone, the new has come!*

If you have made this decision to accept Christ as your Savior, tell someone about it today! (Steps used by permission — Light on the Mountain Ministries)